LET'S CONNECT

kelly jensen

LET'S CONNECT

Cover Art
© 2020 Natasha Snow
https://natashasnow.com/
Cover content is for illustrative purposes only and any person depicted on the cover is a model.

Interior Art
© 2020 Marie
https://www.instagram.com/marieismissing/

Copy Editor: Alex Whitehall
https://alexwhitehall.com/editing-services/

ISBN: 978-1-950625-13-0
04262021

https://shaggydogproductions.online/

> Online Now

Strom

50-year-old man

Philadelphia, PA, USA

Seeking men 45-55 within 20 miles of Philadelphia, PA

Story…

Relationship Status: Divorced

Have Kids: No

Want Kids: If they're yours, sure. Not looking to decant a fresh human at my age.

Ethnicity: I have the complexion of a mushroom. The inside part.

Body type: Lean—through no fault of my own. I remember to eat vegetables around about the time they're plotting escape from the refrigerator. I walk sometimes and call it hiking.

Height: 5'10" is not short. That's ONE INCH above the average height of North American men.

Faith: I'll respect yours if you respect mine.

Smoker: Nope.

Drinker: Not really.

Favorite…

Song: "Wish You Were Here"

Movie: *2001: A Space Odyssey*

Book: *Hyperion*

The most interesting thing about you…

I've always wanted to own a bookstore, so for my thirtieth birthday, I bought one. Not totally spur of the moment. I don't have that kind of cash. Now that I own a bookstore, I have even less. But being able to inhale the scent of paper every day makes me very happy. What about this makes me interesting? I'm one of the few people I know who is truly satisfied with their choice of career.

Your desert isle keepers are (you get two):

A hammock and a good book.

A perfect date is…

A myth. No one and nothing is perfect. I'd count any date a success where the conversation doesn't suck and neither of us gets food poisoning. On a deeper level, though, I think a good date is something like a good book. You've read the cover, you've got an idea what to expect, and at the end of the night, you feel positive about the whole experience. You'd read that author again. A great date is when you've bought the next book before finishing the first.

First Date

Dan straightened his tie, pursed his lips, and turned side to side, checking his face for dried toothpaste. All clear. He cupped his hand in front of his mouth. Fresh breath, check. Smooth shave, yep. Hair—

"Damn it."

Poked himself in the eye? Done.

Bracing his hands against the marble counter in front of the mirror, Dan waited until the pain in his eye receded to a manageable level. Then he squinted at his reflection again. His left eye, an unremarkable brown, was a little watery. His right eye—also brown—was red and watery. He looked as though he'd smoked a fat doobie before coming into the restaurant. And the hair he'd tried to push away from his face? Still curling across his forehead.

Carefully, very carefully, he combed the wayward hank of light brown and gray back, and watched, dismayed, as it flopped forward again.

Hair? Good as it got. Also, the tie looked stupid. He wasn't at a booksellers' convention. He had a date. With someone he didn't know. Someone who had, quite possibly, arrived at the restaurant while Dan lurked in front of the bathroom mirror poking himself in the eye.

He unknotted the tie and stood there with it slung across his palm, wondering what to do with it. Pocket? His slacks were relatively fitted. His nicest pair. Should he unbutton the collar of his shirt? After slinging the tie over his shoulder, Dan unbuttoned the top two buttons, then a third, and then rebuttoned the third. Paused the playback on his reflection, trying to remember if unbuttoning the third had exposed enough skin to make him blush all over. Was it hot in here?

He retrieved the tie, wrapped it around his hand, and mopped his forehead with it.

Oh God. Oh God. Fuck in Heaven. Hallowed whatever. What the actual everything was he doing here? “I can’t do this.”

“Believe in yourself.”

A toilet flushed. The stall door opened a few seconds later, and a middle-aged man strolled out. He had his head down as he tucked his shirt back into his trousers, and one of the recessed spots lighting the bathroom glanced off
of his bald crown. The man looked up and showed Dan a warm smile, and a sense of premonition crept across Dan’s skin.

“Dan?” The guy tilted his head, his smile freezing in place.

“Harold?”

“Yeah!” Harold stuck out a hand and immediately retracted it. “Sorry. Let me just...” He gestured toward the sinks.

Dan shuffled to the side, exposing the length of counter that had been holding him up for the past five minutes. The five minutes Harold had been sitting in a bathroom stall listening to Dan argue with himself.

What had he said out loud?

Also, seriously? Dan glanced toward the ceiling, blinding himself with another of the lights. This was how his first date in seven years was going to start? In a bathroom, with a suspicious odor wafting out of a recently abandoned stall?

Harold had managed to move toward the dryers and was busy waving his hands beneath a feeble stream of air. “I can’t say as I’ve ever met a date in a bathroom before. Definitely a first.”

Dan’s smile felt as weak as the air from the dryer. “Same.”

With a last wave of his hands, Harold extended the right. “How do you do?”

Dan accepted the shake, only realizing he had a tie wrapped around his palm as their hands met. "Oh, um. I looked up the dress code online and there wasn't one, so I googled pictures of the place and a lot of people were wearing ties, so I thought I should wear one. Of course, when I got here, I figured out I'd probably been looking at pictures of a Friday night, not a Saturday night and that all the guys wearing ties had probably just finished work, and, well..."

He was still shaking Harold's hand. Cheeks burning beneath a blush likely as fierce as the red rimming his right eye, Dan yanked his hand back to his side and then shoved it into his pocket. Still wrapped up in his tie. He could feel the bulge. His trousers weren't made for hand-in-pocket poses. Definitely not designed for hand-wrapped-in-tie-and-shoved-in-pocket poses.

Fuck.

He had a better vocabulary. Really, he did. Obviously, he'd left it at Little Volume, his Germantown Avenue bookshop, along with a well-creased copy of *Hyperion*. It was his fifth time reading it. Never got old. In fact, he'd rather be there reading it now.

"Sorry." Dan cleared his throat. "I'm anxious."

Harold's smile was generous. The kindness of his face had been a deciding factor in Dan accepting the date. He and Harold hadn't been chatting for long. Two weeks, if they counted today. And their sporadic exchanges hadn't lit a fire inside Dan. He hadn't come out tonight expecting to fall in love. Or even to have sex. But the reality of Harold's face was... There had to be a more considerate word than *disappointing*.

After running through his mental thesaurus, Dan concluded there wasn't.

"It's all good," Harold said. "I'm a bit anxious as well." He darted a glance toward his recently abandoned stall. "As you can probably tell."

Please let us not discuss his irritable—

"IBS," Harold was saying. "I've been taking something for it, but it's not working. Believe me, this is not how I wanted our date to start."

Dan huffed out a short laugh. "Oh, I can imagine." Really? "What does your doctor say?" Again, really? *Who are you and what have you done with Dan?*

"This is the third drug I've tried, and none of them deal with the spasticity of my colon. We're going to do more tests."

That's great. Just great.

"Oh, well, Um... Good luck with that." It was like talking to a stranger, which felt weird until Dan acknowledged he *was* talking to a stranger, albeit one he'd spent two weeks chatting with online. "Um"—*use your words*—"I don't think this is going to work out."

Maybe not those words.

Harold's face performed a classic fall.

"I'm sorry," Dan hurtled on. "It's me, not you. I don't think I'm ready." The fact he'd never be ready to stand in a funky cloud discussing spastic colons with anyone aside, he wasn't ready for this. For face-to-face conversation.

"I see."

"I'm sorry."

Features twisting somewhere between pain and disappointment, the middle setting an expression Dan would not soon forget, Harold nodded. "Okay. It was nice to meet you?"

"Likewise." Tucking his chin to his chest, Dan turned for the door. It was time to go, before this got any more awkward or depressing. He should leave. But... Quickly, he turned back. "Thanks for taking a chance on me. I hope your next date turns out better."

The memory of Harold's sad smile that Dan took with him was hardly any better. But, hey, he'd saved both of them the expense of dinner, right? And the conversation that would have happened afterward, when one or the other of them, fueled by too much wine, made a clumsy pass.

Dan squeezed his eyes shut, ran into a wall, and swallowed a loud expletive. When he opened his eyes, he was facing another mirror. This one mounted on the wall facing the hostess station. In it, approximately seventy-eight eyeballs were pointed in his direction. Like, the entire restaurant. He lifted his hand—still wrapped in a tie—in a feeble wave.

"Sorry."

Oh, for God's sake.

Turning a final time, Dan sought the front door and fled the restaurant.

An hour later, dressed in pilled gray sweatpants and a Penn State sweatshirt, feet cozied inside thick wooly socks and propped up on the coffee table, Dan opened his laptop across his thighs and logged on to Let's Connect. A greasy feeling circled his empty stomach as he navigated to his connections and deleted HairyGuy aka Harold. That he should have been warned by Harold's choice of username had come up—in conversation with himself and Trevor, upon whom responsibility for this travesty ultimately rested. Trevor had been the one to encourage Dan to try a dating app.

As he hooked his fingers on the top of the screen, ready to shut the laptop, he noted a new connection request. The greasy feeling became an uncomfortable burn. What if that was Harold trying to reconnect? No. He wouldn't, would he? Dan had pretty much dumped him in a bathroom. Not that they'd actually been dating—though the site did suggest their online conversation counted.

Shaking off a swirl of confused thought, Dan shut the laptop and cast it aside. He turned on the TV, lowered the volume, and picked up his phone to send a quick text to his best friend and soul mate, the guy he should be dating, but had missed out on by several years.

Dan: *You round?*

Three dots instantly danced beneath Dan's message.

Trev: *Totally square, man. Always.*

Dan's grin felt good, as though universal balance had been restored.

Dan: *You are.*

Trev: *Are you home already?*

Dan: *We met in a bathroom.*

Trev: ...

Dan: *Not on purpose. He was dealing with a spastic colon, which I had to hear about, and smell, while we made intros. So not ready for that level of intimacy.*

Trev: *Wow. Srsly?*

Dan: *You'd think I was making this up. Unfortunately, I am not.*

The three dots danced and disappeared a couple of times, indicating Trevor was searching for an appropriate reply. Or simply typing one word and laughing. Dan lifted his gaze to the TV and watched a commercial for gutter guards. Feeling vulnerable and disappointed, he was on the verge of making an appointment for his free estimate when his phone buzzed in his hand. He woke the screen.

Trev: *I typed out and deleted about six tasteless jokes. I mean, gay guys aren't afraid to talk about their asses, but he could have at least waited for the coffee course. It's probably for the best. You wouldn't want to go there after a conversation like that.*

Reasonably sure he knew what Trevor meant by *go there*, Dan responded with a *Yeah, no.*

Trev: *Who's next on the list?*

Dan: *I don't know and I don't care. I'm going to take a break from it all, I think.*

Trev: *Nooo. Don't do that. You need to get back up on your horse.*

Dan: *There is no horse, only a sad and divorced fifty-year-old who is quite happy alone.*

Liar.

Well, the sad and divorced parts were true.

Trev: *We talked this through. It's time. You need to start dating again. Spending every night watching Fast and Furious movies and playing Watch Dogs is NOT GOOD FOR YOUR MENTAL HEALTH.*

Dan: *You're here with me at least half of the time. Maybe more.*

Trevor had a boyfriend, but their relationship spanned the continental United States, with Trevor being located in Philly and his other half outside of Oakland, CA.

Trev: *I'm an amazing friend.*

Dan: *You are.*

Trev: *Take the rest of the night off. Go raid a gang hideout in WD and sleep the sleep of the righteous. Start fresh tomorrow.*

Dan: *Yeah.*

After sending a sign off full of random emojis, Dan put the phone aside. The PlayStation controllers were plugged into a charger on the TV console, which suddenly seemed too far away. Like, would need to pack a lunch and wear sensible shoes distance. Sighing, flopping his head into the cushy part of the couch behind him, Dan closed his eyes and played games in his head instead. Games where he'd have woken up to the lying, cheating, and bastardry two months earlier than he had. Then he might not have had to go through his divorce alone.

Trevor had been away—invited to lecture for a semester on the opposite coast—and Dan had been bored enough to wake up to the fact he was married in name only. The desiccated condoms he'd found under the bed only confirmed it.

What Dan could never decide was whether the demise of his marriage had been his fault or not. If he'd been more present, would he and Chris still be together? Thoughts like that always brought up deeper and more disappointed chains, though, the links of which he'd told himself to let go time and time again. Dan had met Trevor only hours before he'd met Chris. If they hadn't gone out that night, all of them…

Stop. Just stop.

He and Trevor were meant to be friends. That was how things had worked out.

Dan opened his eyes, levered his lean frame off the couch, and retrieved a controller from the charging station. Trevor was right. Trevor was always right. Dispensing some virtual albeit questionable justice might be exactly what he needed.

For tonight.

Second Date

Dan propped his feet on the coffee table. Instead of reaching for the remote or PlayStation controller, he picked up his phone, ready to get his second date postmortem with Trevor out of the way. It would be short and sweet. Dan had spent forty-five minutes freezing his ass off outside a bar on Germantown Avenue, waiting for no one to arrive. Yes, he'd texted his prospective date. No, he hadn't wanted to wait inside. The place hadn't been crowded enough for him to drink alone and not be noticed.

Stupid, maybe, but it was what it was.

Before confessing all to Trevor, Dan checked Let's Connect one last time to see if BilliardBalls (what was with these names?) had sent him a message. According to the app, their connection no longer existed.

Great. Terrific. Fan-fucking-tastic.

The guy had probably seen him outside the bar and decided not to meet up. Had it been the lack of tie? The enticing aroma of old books? Then, instead of sending a polite *Hey, this isn't going to work out*, he'd deleted their connection and disappeared.

Who did that?

If Dan could summon the whatever to turn a guy down in a restaurant bathroom, BilliardBalls could have...

Eh, whatever.

He texted his woes to Trevor, who did not respond.

Where was he? Trevor never went out; he didn't need to.

Oh... Was he currently sexting or whatnot with his boyfriend?

Dan closed his eyes. When a porn reel of Trevor and Kevin—who would forever remain blurry-faced because, for some reason, Trevor had never shared a picture of him—started up, he opened them again. Nope. Not going there. Never.

He was watching an infomercial for wool dryer balls (and about to order one) when his phone buzzed.

He'd downloaded the Let's Connect mobile app before his date, and the chat bubble had a new notification. Dan opened his inbox.

Robin wants to connect.

Robin? The image of a small, red-breasted bird popped into his head, no doubt prompted by the similar avian set as Robin's avatar. Interesting choice. Most users went with, you know, a headshot. Sometimes they posted a ripped (or unfortunately flabby) torso. Dick picks were discouraged, but the odd one slipped past. Birds? Nope.

Nevertheless, Dan clicked through to Robin's deets. He was forty-nine years old, five feet, eleven inches tall, and had chosen *average build*, which could mean anything. He'd checked *employed*, but hadn't shared in which industry. He had, however, answered the three questions that made up the most interesting part of any profile.

A user could lie about their height and weight, or whether they smoked or drank (Robin did neither), and anyone could pick a cool song or movie as their favorite. Well, most people could. Robin's was *The Dark Knight*, which only made his choice of username ever more interesting.

The three questions required a minimum of fifty words in answer. They required more thought, or so Dan liked to think.

To the question *What's the most interesting thing about you?* Robin had answered:

My sock collection. I never throw away the lost socks, the laundry orphans, the singular but proud refugees who migrate from someone else's basket to mine, the war veterans, the random keepers who only want a family and a home. I keep them all. I wear them, too. Matching them as closely as I can to another sock, forming new pairs, thus ensuring each and every sock in my possession has at least a chance of finding their happy ever after.

Robin's short essay on socks was probably the most bizarre yet sweet collection of words Dan had ever read. Surely a man who gave a home to lost socks could find a place in his heart for an old, sad, and divorced specimen of hosiery like Dan.

You are not a sock, Daniel.

Whatever.

Dan moved on to the second question. *Your desert isle keepers are (you get two)?*

Answers to this one usually fell into one of three categories. The smartasses took boats, planes, helicopters, or satellite radios with them. They weren't interested in being stuck on an island in the middle of nowhere with no means of escape. They were the go-getters and overachievers. The sort of people who'd let a man wait outside a bar for forty-five minutes in March. The dreamers took knives and rope to build treehouses and plan irrigation systems. They were going to Robinson-Crusoe the heck out of that island before they constructed a boat out of palm fronds, coconut shells, and the bones of small monkeys. They didn't want to be on the island either.

The last group included people like Dan—the folks who figured the question was purely metaphorical and didn't sweat it. Much. Dan was on his island with a hammock and a good book. He had agonized over which book to take before finally settling on "a good book." Wasn't like he was actually going there anyway, and if he was, then the island gods could surprise him.

Robin's answer fell into the same category. He'd written:

You. We'll either a) kill each other (and let's not talk about what we'd do with the body—we'll assume there's another food source on the island. Actually, wait, let's talk about the body. I'd like to think I'd give you a decent burial. I'd compose a poem for your funeral. I'd be sorry I killed you.) or b) get to know each other really, really well. Where else would we find the time and space to talk? Not at a bar, that's for sure. For the record? I prefer option b.

Dan flopped back into the pillows he kept in his cozy couch corner and nestled for a little while, his phone a warm rectangle in his hand. The screen had darkened by the time he got settled, and he made no attempt to wake it. His mind was too full of lost socks and broad expanses of sand. Of hammocks big enough for two, and how utterly amazing it would be to have a companion who wanted to do nothing but watch the sun rise and set, listen to the waves sigh against the shore, and talk. Or not. To just be, maybe. Absorb each other's energy, to actually feel the other's presence.

Man, that'd be nice. Dan was ready to pack his bags.

Could it be that what he needed was a vacation? Not a date, not a partner, but an escape. Of course, if he did go away alone, he'd probably swing in a damned hammock alone, and then he'd come home alone, and end up in this same corner of the couch, surrounded by pillows and alone.

"You're forgetting one important fact," he told himself. "Robin, the guy of lost socks and endless sunsets, wants to connect."

A thrill lit up his insides. How, out of all the lonely people on Let's Connect, had Robin selected him? Robin was either new to the site or had been disappointed a hundred times previously.

Dan woke the phone and cheed out the third question. He was ready to accept the connection request now, but curiosity regarding Robin's idea of a perfect date won out.

You're probably expecting me to say Hawaii, and you're probably expecting me to be wearing my mismatched socks and a soulful smile. Or maybe you're thinking I'm a stay-at-home guy. That I'm going to offer to cook for you and invite you to watch a movie afterward. Only we'd never get to the movie because I've got condoms and lube in a drawer under the coffee table. Better yet, you're imagining I'm a fancy-restaurant kind of guy. That I want to meet you somewhere that has a balcony from where we can watch the sun set and assess each other in the most flattering light.

I'm not a nightclub guy. I'm not the guy who will meet you outside a bar. I'm not going to suggest something different but cute, like going to the zoo or checking out the latest exhibit at the Franklin Institute.

Here's where I'm going to get really honest, and here's where you're going to decide whether or not we'll connect. I've been hurt before. You have too. So, all we're going to do is talk. Me at my place, you at yours. We're going to attempt to connect, in the truest sense of the word. Maybe we'll watch a movie together one night, me on my couch, you on yours. Let's pick a language and practice speaking to each other using all the wrong words. Let's play Scrabble online, using our own rules. All of your words have to be things in your house. Mine will be the same.

What do you want to do on our date?

"Wow."

Who was this guy? He couldn't possibly be real. Also, Dan had the sudden urge to edit his profile, except nothing he'd ever write could possibly measure up. Then again, Robin had requested a connection, which meant he'd already read Dan's answers. Heartbeat fluttering near his esophagus, Dan navigated back to the chat bubble and accepted Robin's request.

A chat window opened with the usual warning hovering over the top, advising users not to share personal information, blah, blah, blah. Dan dismissed the warning and stared at the blank screen. He typed *Hi*, deleted it, typed it again, deleted it a second time, and put his phone aside.

He was too tired to be witty tonight.

But, having accepted the connection, he felt obligated to say something, even if it was along the lines of: *I'm too tired to be witty tonight.*

"Don't type that. God."

Dan chewed on his lip. Worried a shred of dead skin with his tongue, fished a ChapStick out of his sweatpants pocket, and smoothed it back down. Winter was a cold, icy, dry bitch. He sighed. Opened the notepad app on his phone and fought his thumbs and autocorrect for ten minutes, finally producing what he thought might be a reasonable parley. The beginning of one.

Thanks for the connection request. I'll admit I'm a little intimidated by your profile. You're obviously much more interesting then me.

Damn it. He highlighted *then* and replaced it with *than.*

...much more interesting than me.

No, that was terrible. He sounded too...

"Be more confident, Dan."

Thanks for the connection request!

To exclaim or not to exclaim?

Dan deleted the exclamation point.

Thanks for the connection request. Love your profile. Super thoughtful, dude.

"'Dude'?"

Thanks for the connection request. Love your profile.

No.

Thanks for the... "Shit."

After casting the phone aside, Dan pressed the heels of his palms into his eyes. Orange and purple blobs merged behind his closed lids, and a headache knocked quietly on the back of his skull. He was tired. And discouraged. And feeling severely outclassed. But he didn't want to leave the connection dangling. What if he woke up tomorrow to find it gone?

He picked up his phone and started again.

Hi. I've been sitting here for like half an hour typing and deleting responses to your connection request. Your profile sets the bar high, and I'm pretty sure nothing I say will be good enough. But I figure you asked to connect for a reason, that something you read in my profile sparked a level of interest. All's not lost, right?

What I like about your profile is how different it is, without being... I dunno. I want to say elitist. You come across as intelligent, but not on yourself. I'm sure there's a better word for that, but it's late and I'm tired.

I spent 45 mins outside a bar tonight, waiting for a guy who either showed up, took one look at me, and fled, or who got cold feet, or... I dunno. I say that a lot. Fair warning. I also swear.

Anyway, let's—drumroll, please—connect. I know. It's not even a real pun. That's me. I'm going to switch off my phone and go to bed now, because this has been a super stressful evening already and I...

"What the fuck are you doing?"

Dan read over what he'd written. It was terrible. But it was also honest. It sounded like him. Worst case, Robin would read it and break the connection. Best case? They'd keep talking. Either way, this was Dan. The sooner Robin realized that the better.

"Who am I kidding?"

No one, Dan. You're kidding no one.

He finished typing:

...want to be more collected next time we talk.

Okay. Not the greatest message ever, but he'd already argued with himself long enough. How to sign off, though? Not *Best*, not *Take care*, not *Sweet dreams*.

He finally typed:

Chat with you then.

After cutting and pasting the message into the app, Dan switched off his phone and plugged it into the charger in the kitchen.

Dan

Third Date

Waiting for Robin to respond became waiting for the sun to rise, for the mail to arrive, for someone to buy the pristine, signed collection of Stephen King novels mounted like rare butterflies in the glass case beneath the register.

Dan would have a hard time parting with the 1987 first edition *Misery*, even though he had another one shelved upstairs in his apartment. Same went for all four books of the Hyperion Cantos. For all the beauties trapped in his cage.

The bell over the front door jangled, and Dan pointed his best gaze forward—the one of bored attention that let customers know he was there, but not going to interfere. Book people liked their space. They either wanted to browse aimlessly or hunt specific prey. They'd come to him if they needed assistance.

He shifted his buttocks on the stool he kept behind the counter and picked up the well-thumbed Don Winslow doorstop he'd borrowed from the bargain shelf. America's war on drugs failed to hold his attention, though. His eyes felt gritty and a mysterious pain ghosted his spine. He hadn't been sleeping well. His phone battery kept running low at odd times. Relentless monitoring of his Let's Connect inbox, no doubt.

After checking whether his lone customer was still browsing, Dan put the book aside to wake his phone… and froze midbreath, lungs half-filled, at the sight of a little red notification over the app's chat bubble. Had Robin finally responded? Or was someone else requesting a connection? Either possibility filled him with an emotion he couldn't quite name.

Maybe he should delete the app.

Movement caught his eye—his customer roving from bestsellers to horror. Dan tapped the chat bubble. The note was from Robin.

Are you sitting down?

Yes, but why? Oh God, he wasn't going to get dumped before they ever got a chance to properly talk, was he?

Dan read on.

Just checking that you're comfortable because you might be here for a while.

He might? Dan scrolled forward to check the length of the note and found it ended after three paragraphs. He'd be done reading in about a minute. He scrolled back to the top.

First and foremost, I enjoyed your note. I imagined you writing it out about six times, deleting it, and then delivering it with a fatalistic smile, figuring I'd either see it for what it was, or... not. Were you secretly hoping for the not?

Okay, I'm going to stop addressing you as if you might respond, because right now our conversation is one dimensional. I'd like to take it to the second dimension. Let's (drumroll, please) connect. Our places, tonight, around eight?

I know you were expecting a longer note. Either that, or you checked how long it was and are now wondering why I asked if you were sitting down. Or why I figured you'd be here for a while. You're going to read this over, this inconsequential note, several times. How do I know this? Because that's what I did with yours.

Chat soon.

Huh.

Dan checked the time: 3:15 p.m. Four hours and forty-five minutes (or so) until their scheduled chat. Was that unsettled feeling in his gut excitement or hunger? Dan glanced at the balled-up sandwich wrapper lurking next to the trash can. Though lunch was a fading memory, it wasn't a need for food that gripped him. It was apprehension. The tone of Robin's note confused him. Even disturbed him a little. Why would Robin assume he'd have to read it over six times? Who was this arrogant ass?

Feeling put off, Dan set the phone aside and picked up his book.

His customer arrived at the counter thirty seconds later with a stack of horror novels. Even without the familiarity of her face and the woolly hat stuffed with bulky braids, Dan would have known her by the lingering gaze she cast in the direction of the Stephen King novels lined up beneath the glass.

Dan gave her a smile. "Still here waiting for you, Heather."

Heather smiled back. "One day." Nudging her stack forward, she opened the bidding at, "Can I get five for three?"

"That's the Sunday deal, and only for the bargain table."

"But I can't be here on Sunday and you never put anything good on the bargain table."

Dan held up his Don Winslow. "This is pretty good."

She wrinkled her nose. "How about five for four?"

Pulling a long-suffering sigh up from the floor, Dan pretended to think on it. They both knew he'd say yes. That she hadn't started with fifty cents each meant she was in a hurry. Dan held out a hand, she pulled a rumpled fold of bills from one of the many pockets on her coat.

"Need a bag?" Dan asked.

"Nope!" She picked up her books with the expression of someone who was thinking about kissing them but had decided to wait until she left the store. "See you next week!"

"See you then."

The hours until six—when he normally closed—passed slowly. Dan picked up his phone and read Robin's note again. Maybe Robin was as anxious as he'd been. Maybe he came across as a bit of an asshole when he was nervous. On the third read, Dan decided exactly that.

At six, he flipped the closed sign, locked the door, turned off the lights, and set the alarm before beginning his long commute up the back stairs. His apartment was warm and cozy. The corner of the couch beckoned. Dan fixed himself a plate of leftovers first and then forced himself to eat while he considered entertainment possibilities. Netflix, HSN, PlayStation?

Folks always assumed he spent his evenings reading. He read all day. At night, he wanted to rest his eyes. Trevor got it. Trevor spent most of his day reading too. A wrinkle marred Dan's brow as he thought of his friend. He and Trevor hadn't exchanged more than a passing text over the past week, and they hadn't spent an evening together since that night in February when Trevor had insisted Dan needed to start dating again.

At eight o'clock, Dan's phone buzzed, surprising him. Shaking away thoughts and vague weariness, Dan opened the Let's Connect chat app and watched as Robin's first live message appeared.

Robin: *Hey there.*

Dan waited a full minute before typing back: *Hi.*

Robin: *You're here.*

Dan: *I'm here.*

Robin: *Thank Christ—or whoever you believe in. I was wondering if you'd show.*

Dan: *I was wondering if you were going to show.*

Robin: *Is our whole conversation going to be you echoing my thoughts? Because there's a chat bot that does that.*

Offended, Dan put his phone down. He chewed on his lip until the screen darkened and switched off. Contemplated the weird feeling in his gut. *Again*. The phone vibrated softly under his palm, and he woke the screen.

Robin: *Sorry. That came out wrong. I'm nervous.*

Three dots pulsed beneath the message bubble. Dan waited for the rest of it.

Robin: *I worked on my profile answers for a long time, and now I kind of wish I hadn't, because I sound witty and put together there, and that's difficult to replicate in real time, or on demand, or even in response.*

Dan's mouth crooked up on one side.

Dan: *I get it. If it's any comfort, I did type out my response to your connection request about six times in a notepad app before I copied it over.*

Robin: *THAT IS A COMFORT. Thank you.*

Dan: *You're welcome.*

Robin: *Okay, it's our first date. What are we going to talk about?*

Dan: *The awful dates that came before. It's, like, a rule.*

Robin: *Lol. Sure. You're going to have to start, though, because this is my first date on the app.*

Dan: *You're kidding?*

Robin: *Nope.*

Dan: *And you chose ME?*

Three dots appeared and disappeared under Dan's last bubble for a while. For long enough that Dan picked at the cold leftovers on the side of his plate and thought about getting something to drink.

Finally, Robin's reply appeared.

Robin: *I did.*

That was it? It had taken Robin nearly four minutes to type *I did*? Obviously he'd typed something else, deleted it, something after that, deleted it, and probably even a couple of somethings after that.

Dan: *Why?*

Robin: *Because I wanted to talk to you.*

Exhaling slowly, Dan nestled back into the cozy corner of the couch and propped his feet. Then he put his thumbs to the keyboard on his phone.

Dan: *Okay. I already told you about the bar. That was my last date. The second I got through this site. The one before that was actually worse in that I met the guy in the bathroom. He was experiencing gastro intestinal issues, and I pretty much fast-forwarded to the point where he'd expect me to live with said issues, and I wasn't sure I was up for that. I mean, I guess if you really love someone, you don't care if they stink up your bathroom on the regular, but I wasn't ready to go there, mentally or physically. Not yet. I just...*

Chewing on his lip again, Dan read over what he'd written and continued.

...I want to get to know someone before I even start thinking in terms of a relationship. Or sex. I'm lonely, but not that lonely, if that makes sense.

He hit send and melted back into the couch to wait for Robin's reply.

On the TV, an ad for solar path lights filled the space until his phone vibrated against his palm.

Robin: *I get it. Trust me, I do. Talking is seriously underrated. Ironically, that's supposed to be the point of apps like this. For us to talk and get to know each other before we connect in person. Of course, with every second person, or even three out of five or, say, eight out of ten pretending it's a less gritty version of a hookup app, there probably isn't a lot of talking getting done. By the way, I find it easier to type out numbers than find the digit in the number line. How about you?*

Dan: *Definitely easier to type out the numbers. Even with my thumbs. Excuse any and all typos, btw.*

Robin: *Of course. Same here. Can I ask how long you've been single?*

The three dots danced, and Dan waited them out.

Robin: *You are single, right?*

Dan: *I am. I'm divorced. It's been a little over a year. I'm on this app because my best friend was sick of hearing me mope. To be honest, I'm not sure if I'm ready.*

Robin's return message seemed to be taking a while. Dan put the phone aside again and took his empty plate back into the kitchen. He filled the electric kettle and spent the time waiting for it to boil sorting through the herbal tea options in the cabinet over the counter. By the time he got back to the couch with a cup of something vaguely minty, Robin had replied.

Robin: *Who is? Getting together with another human is altogether weird, when you think about it. And if you're going to do that, think about it, then you're probably going to look at the relationships in your periphery, the successes and failures. They're all different. No one really knows, even inside a relationship, what truly makes it work. I've watched a marriage fall apart and thought to myself, how did they even last this long? They were never right for each other. I couldn't understand how they got together. I figured it had to be the sex. Or maybe it was an issue of convenience—sex and companionship. Both worked out okay and they settled.*

The skin along Dan's arms prickled. His cheeks warmed. He undid the top button on his shirt and loosened the collar a little. Robin couldn't possibly know how close to the bone he'd sliced. Then again, maybe he did. Maybe he was speaking from the heart.

A nasty thought occurred. He wasn't talking to his ex-husband, was he?

Dan flipped back to Robin's profile and checked his location again. *Philly area.*

Dan's prickles prickled. His face was hot. No. Fate would never be so unkind. Dan flipped to his own profile. As though he'd been jabbed by a sharp needle, air wheezed out of him. There was no way his ex could mistake Dan's profile for anything other than Dan's profile, from the username—Strom, which was a shortened version of his surname, Stroman—to the clearly recognizable photo.

Unless.

No. Just no. Dan had debased himself during their divorce.

Thinking about it now stirred up the leftovers in Dan's stomach. What a fool he'd been. He'd rather have been in a dysfunctional relationship than alone. Not anymore, though. No longer.

Robin: *You still there?*

Dan: *Checking your profile to make sure you're not my ex.*

Robin: *Should I lol or sign off?*

Dan: *Sorry. This is...*

What?

Dan: *You're right. Getting together with another person is weird when you think about it. What is it that makes two people compatible? I mean, your profile rocks. After I read it, I felt like I kind of knew you, but not. I wanted to get to know you better. And our chat tonight has been... can I say challenging? But I like that too. I like that you're making me think and feel. It's good. But it's also uncomfortable and I don't know if I'm ready for that.*

Robin: *I know.*

Dan: *What does that mean?*

Robin: *It means I feel the same way. This isn't going how I expected it to.*

Dan: *How did you expect it to go?*

Robin: *I figured we'd toss a conversational beach ball back and forth, watching it spin and shine in the sun between punts. That our banter would be worthy of an episode of Gilmore Girls. That I'd sound like I'd been scripted by Alan Sorkin. Alas, it is not so. I keep putting my metaphorical foot in my mouth and you're surprisingly human.*

Dan: *Ah, thanks?*

Robin: *Yw*

Dan: *Can I ask how long you've been single?*

Robin's reply didn't bounce straight back. Neither did the three dots dance. Dan pictured Robin on his own couch, staring at his phone, thinking. Chewing his lower lip, maybe. Dan stopped chewing on his. He picked up the remote and killed the TV, tired of the constant stream of consumerism playing in the background. If Robin was feeling as lightly bruised as Dan was, the end of their conversation was close. The end of this date.

Dan wasn't sure if they'd schedule another, and he wasn't sure how he felt about that.

Finally, Robin's response lit up the screen.

Robin: *I'd call it a biblically long time, but... it's been a while. Years. There was someone a couple of years ago. It didn't last. My fault. I wasn't committed. My thoughts were elsewhere and he could tell.*

Elsewhere had to mean with another person.

Robin: *Are you feeling like the peach that escaped the shopping bag and ended up under the car, wedged against a tire, ready to be squashed flat?*

A grin edged across Dan's mouth as he typed: *So much like that peach.*

Robin: *Want to call it a night?*

Dan hesitated with his thumbs over the small keyboard, grin stiff, one side of his mouth twitching. After about a minute, he typed: *Sure. Can we chat again?*

Robin: *I'd like that.*

Dan: *How about Saturday night? Are you free? I could send you a recipe. We'll both cook it. You can choose the movie. How's eight sound?*

Robin: *You're surprisingly good at this.*

Dan: *Should I be offended by your surprise?*
Robin: *No. Be… delighted. I am.*
Dan: [cheesy grin emoji] *Chat with you on Saturday.*
Robin: *Chat with you then.*

Fourth Date

Coffee dates were like middle children. They sounded innocuous. What could happen in a coffee shop? But they could be devious. What couldn't happen in a coffee shop?

Standing outside the men's bathroom, shaking coffee from his hand, Dan stared mournfully at his shirt sleeve, sure the stain would never come out. He also harbored some trepidation regarding the current occupant of the bathroom. Was it his date? Would they emerge on a cloud of ill-scented air? This was his fate, wasn't it? Dates met in bathrooms, outside of bathrooms, going into bathrooms. A fast-forward to what his life with this particular person might be.

Oh, God. Why?

The door opened and a teenager sauntered out, not meeting Dan's eyes.

Dan grabbed the door before it closed—the code for the lock had melted with his receipt—and hurriedly shut himself inside. He washed his hands, splashed water over his sleeve, and avoided the mirror. Nothing good ever came from looking in the mirror. Besides, he hadn't had time to get changed, so it was bookshop chic or nothing.

Hands washed, shirt sleeve damp and still stained, he left the bathroom and hurried back to the table in the far corner where he'd left his traitorous cup. An elderly couple sat there. With his cup. It remained center stage, their short and tall cups flanking it.

Was he supposed to take it?

They were, like, at least eighty. You couldn't ask eighty-year-olds to get up and go. You were supposed to give them your table.

Closing his eyes and counting to ten in the middle of a crowded coffee shop would not be a good look. Counting under his breath instead, willing his temper not to tear and fray, Dan reached between them to retrieve his cup.

"Excuse me. Sorry. I left this here."

The male half of the couple looked up at him with watery eyes. "Did we take your table?"

"No! No. It's all good." Dan raised his cup in a short salute. "Have a nice day."

A throat cleared behind him. Dan turned. A young woman with more facial piercings than should be healthy stood there holding a cardboard cup of her own.

"Are you Strom?"

"I am."

"I'm supposed to give this to you." The silver ball on her tongue mesmerized him. "He said he had to go, but felt bad, so here's a coffee." She thrust the cup forward. "Something like that. I mean, it's not like he had me repeat it or anything. Or paid me." Her eyes narrowed with the effect of aiming the dagger points of her eyebrow piercings at him. "He said—"

Dan snatched the cup. Unfortunately, the speed with which he did the snatching, combined with the pressure of his grip, popped the plastic top off. Hot coffee splashed over his hand and up on his shirt sleeve. Again.

"Goddamn it!"

The young woman backed up a step. The older couple at the table leaned toward the wall. Every other head in the café turned in Dan's direction and the needle-sharp feeling of too many eyes stabbed at his skin.

Fuck my life.

Coffee cup in either hand and clenching his teeth together hard enough to grind his molars into dust, Dan swept out of the store. The other lid abandoned him somewhere along the way. By the time he got to his car, both of his hands were covered in coffee, creamer, sugar, and something that felt a lot like self-pity. Dan tried snarling at the parking meter, but couldn't pull it off. He wanted to go. He set the cups down on the curb, determined not to take them with him, and straightened. What was that on his windshield? A parking ticket? What? He'd…

The meter stood in defiance to his second snarl, blinking merrily away. Empty. The meter next door? Oh, that one was full. Dan felt like spitting at the car in front of it.

Enjoy your free parking, asshole!

It was an older model car, boatlike with its wide hood and pointy rear light fixtures. Probably belonged to the older couple who'd taken his table.

Dan ripped the ticket out from beneath the wiper, stuffed it into his pocket, and got into his car. He almost screamed at a tap on the window. It was a traffic cop. In her hands were his two abandoned coffee cups.

"You forgot these!"

Dan: *I don't know if I have the mental capacity for Saturday night. Sorry for the late notice, but I need to take a break from this whole dating thing.*

Robin: *I understand.*

That was it? Dan had waited an hour for *I understand*?

No, his mood had not improved. In fact, since arriving back at the store, it had continued spiraling downward with no end in sight. Not usually prone to depression—he had moods, often shaken off after a day of wallowing—Dan wondered whether age was finally messing with his brain chemistry or whether his current mood was another passing phase.

Maybe tomorrow he would feel like dating again.

Maybe he was better off alone.

Retrieving a sigh from his lungs, he hauled it upward and outward. Alone didn't have to mean lonely, did it?

He woke his phone and texted Trevor. *I hate you.*

Trevor responded right away. *What did I do now?*

Dan: *You hassled me into this dating thing and it sucks. All of it. Everything sucks. The world sucks. The universe is one big sucking black hole.*

Trev: *Did you get stood up again?*

Dan: *Is it me, or is it me?*

Trev: *Will you hit me if I say it's you? J/k. It's totally them. Always them. I mean, you're the one showing up, right? So it's them.*

Dan: *They're leaving after seeing me, though.*

Dan looked down at his creased khakis and stained shirt. Beneath, lay the body of a fifty-year-old. Dan didn't feel fifty… except in the mornings, and on the rare occasion he indulged in day drinking, which usually resulted in an afternoon nap of mammoth proportions and a sleepless night, leaving him cranky and feeling about sixty the next day.

Right now, he felt too old and too young at the same time. And lonely. And depressed. The stupid part was that he hadn't even been looking forward to the coffee date. He and the guy had only exchanged a couple of messages before agreeing to meet and see. Dan had been more focused on his upcoming evening with Robin but figured meeting someone else for coffee couldn't hurt. If the attraction failed to sizzle, he could always use another friend.

Out of all his failed dates thus far, he hadn't even connected with someone he might hang out with.

Maybe he *was* on the wrong site after all. He should be scrolling through Meetups instead. Finding a new gaming group or a movie group. A group of not-so-old and mildly depressed people looking for new friends.

His phone buzzed in his hand.

Oh, right. He did actually have a friend. One long-suffering but awesomely understanding friend.

Trev: *It's probably too real for them. Chatting online is all well and good, but then they see you're a real person and they can't go through with it. That'd be my take, anyway.*

Dan: *Thanks. And you're probably right. I wouldn't do that. Get cold feet and blow someone off like that. But I can see how—*

Well, damn. He'd done exactly that, exactly ten minutes ago. To Robin.

Dan deleted his unsent text and typed a new one. *I don't think I'm as nice a person as I thought I was.*

Trev: *What do you mean? You're a great person. You're my favorite person!*

Dan: *Your bf isn't your favorite person?*

The three dots danced beneath his reply for a while. Dan waited them out.

Trev: *It's different.*

Dan: *What were you going to say before you deleted it and typed that?*

Trev: *Lol. Busted. I was getting all philosophical and it was weird. It was about how you can love different people for different reasons.*

A cold hand closed over the back of Dan's neck. In his chest, his heart stuttered.

Dan: *You're in love?*

It shouldn't come as a surprise. Trevor had been dating the same guy for well over a year.

Trev: *I am, for all the good it does me.*

Dan: *What does that mean?*

Trev: *Sometimes it's like he's so far away I can't reach him, you know?*

Rather than reply that that was how long-distance relationships tended to go, Dan put down something kinder. Words that tore little pieces of his soul loose, setting them to drift in the current of dry air puffing out of the nearby heating vent.

Dan: *Maybe you should think about moving out there.*

Trev: *I don't know if I'm ready for that. Then again, when have I ever been ready for the big stuff? Sometimes I look back over the decisions I've made, particularly in the past decade, and wonder if I should be allowed to run a life. Or why we weren't given a fucking handbook.*

Dan: *I know, right? What's with turning us out into this world unprepared?*

Trev: *To be fair, we did have parents. Both of us. Nice parents. Both of us.*

Dan smiled. Trevor was right on that score. They'd both won the parent lottery. He should call his mom this weekend. Remind her of that fact.

But back to the matter at hand…

Dan: *If there's one thing I've learned over the past year, it's that…*

What? What exactly had he learned from his divorce?

…I wish I'd taken more chances. That I'd given more of myself. I mean, if I was going to end up alone anyway, wouldn't it have been better to know that I at least made the most of what I had while I had it?

Trevor's reply seemed to take a while. Instead of defaulting to the paperback facedown on the counter, Dan pushed off the stool and took a tour of the store, reshelving some books, visiting others. When had he sold the box set of— Oh, there they were. He tidied and mused until it was time to close the store for the evening.

He was halfway through another plate of scintillating leftovers when he remembered to check his phone.

Trev: *And here they think you can't teach old dogs new tricks.*

Dan huffed out a laugh. While wandering the shop, he'd been thinking about Robin and the quiet but somehow dignified way he'd responded to Dan's abrupt text. About how Robin might have felt. Had Dan trashed their fledgling connection?

He opened Let's Connect, and sent a new note to Robin.

*Hey. Is it too late to say I'm sorry? I had a shitty day and took it out on you. I guess this could count as a preview of what's to come, or maybe it's just a blip. Or maybe it's that I *am* very human and definitely fallible. Anyway, long story short, if you're still interested in getting together—virtually, of course—on Saturday, I'll be here. Have a good night! Dan.*

After he hit send, Dan stared at the name he'd attached to the end of his note. His real, actual name. The message would come from Strom, as all his messages and chats did. But there, at the bottom of the note, he'd given something real.

The sense of panic he wanted to feel sputtered and died. If Robin chose to read between the lines, Dan's real, actual name might be the most convincing word. A gesture. An act of faith. An invitation to more.

Maybe he was ready, after all.

Robin

Fifth Date

Robin: *Okay, this recipe? I had to shop at three different stores to get all the ingredients.*

Dan: *I shopped at one called Tandoor Palace. The delivery guy was pretty cute. I tipped him extra.*

Robin: *You didn't cook?*

Heat that Robin wasn't there to appreciate stung Dan's cheeks.

Dan: *I was going to. It's a pretty easy recipe. You'll have enough stuff for another ten tries btw. I was super busy at the store today, though, and then I remembered Tandoor Palace does the BEST naan bread. Sorry!*

He *had* been busy with regular customers asking for books he didn't have, and new customers hauling in their dead aunt's collection of Reader's Digest condensed novels *and then leaving them* in his store after being politely informed that no one would buy them. Well, one new customer and five smelly old boxes. Dan had dropped them at the nursing home three blocks behind the store and had seen the yet-to-be-lit sign for Tandoor Palace on his way back.

Robin: *If we ever date in person, is this what I can expect? Empty takeout containers in the trash and a cheerful lie about how you slaved all day making my favorite dinner?*

Dan: *Speaking of, what is your favorite dinner?*

Robin: *This curry is pretty good. Tastes nearly as fantastic as the satisfaction of calling three different stores and then spending one and a half hours soaking, rinsing, grinding, and learning how to make ghee.*

Dan: *I feel curiously as if I've been slapped.*

Robin: **satisfied smirk**

Dan: *I'd say this date was going as well as all the others before it, but it's the only one where I've gotten to the dinner portion. So guilt away if it makes you feel better. You're here. We're eating. I'm counting it as a win.*

Robin: *Heh. Just gonna say this once: you shoulda cooked. It was fun and I'd have liked to have heard about whether you used a food processor for the grinding, or one of those mortar and pestle things.*

Dan: *I'd have gone food processor all the way. Or bought ready-ground spices. I'm actually a terrible cook. I have no idea why I suggested we cook for this.*

Robin: *So we'd have something to do with our hands?*

Dan: *I'm currently typing with mine. You?*

Robin: *Point.*

Dan nestled into his cozy couch corner and lifted his feet to the coffee table. He had a plate of various foodstuffs on the cushion beside him, the enticing aroma of curry drifting slowly upward. Regarding the plate, he did feel some measure of guilt. He should have cooked. He also knew that it had been a shitty thing to do to Robin. It was as though he wasn't taking their date seriously. Then again, when a guy refused to meet in person, things were already weird.

Robin: *Do you have the movie cued up?*

Dan: *I do. Want to start watching?*

Robin: *On three.*

The numbers popped up in separate chat bubbles and Dan pressed play when the 3 appeared. Then wondered if Robin was starting with the previews or the actual movie.

Dan: *Did you already watch the previews?*

Robin: *I never watch the previews.*

Dan: *You and my friend both! How can you decide what else to see if you don't watch the previews?*

Robin: *Um... It's available for streaming and I haven't seen it yet?*

Déjà vu tickled Dan's shoulders again. No. Nope. Trevor wouldn't do this to him. Also, probably half of the population of America skipped the previews. They were the folks who thought pineapple shouldn't go on pizza. But, just to test…

Dan: *Pizza toppings. Go.*

Robin: *Anything but pineapple and anchovies.*

Dan: *I don't think this is going to work out. Also, you don't happen to be called Trevor Mackey in real life, do you?*

Robin: *Um, no? Who's that?*

Dan: *The friend I mentioned. I had a sudden panic attack that he was pranking me, somehow. That you were. Which is ridiculous. Trevor would never do that to me. Would he???*

Robin: *Is this were I answer 'no,' thereby confirming that I'm actually this Trevor person? Or do I judiciously remain silent. Btw, autocorrect wanted to do rude things to judiciously.*

Laughing, Dan put his phone aside to eat some of his curry, and with the taste of cumin and coconut resting happily on his tongue and warm food finally sliding toward his belly, the world brightened by several shades.

Dan: *Have you seen this movie before?*

Robin: *About ten times. It's why I chose it. That way we could watch and chat at the same time.*

Dan: *Good choice. Have you seen any of his other films?*

Robin: *If I answer in the affirmative, are you going to accuse me of being your friend in disguise again?*

Dan: *No. But you could be my ex.*

Robin: ...

Dan: *Sorry. My sense of humor was taken off the shelves after I bought it. You can't find it anywhere now.*

Robin: *I'm going to say that's a good thing.*

Dan put his phone aside to eat some more, intending to watch a little of the movie. Instead, he found himself scrolling back through his conversation with Robin, smiling at the flow of banter.

Dan: *I'm going to give us a Gilmore Girls score of seven out of ten for tonight.*

Robin: *Right? We're doing great!*

Grinning, Dan settled back into his cushions. They had an inside joke already, and a fun memory of Dan not cooking while Robin put forth a sterling effort, even making his own curry seasoning. After two dates, they had the building blocks of a relationship. Something shared and a story to tell. Would their in-person chemistry be as good?

Dan: *How long are we going to do this chat thing before you stand me up outside the bathroom in a coffee shop?*

Dan watched as his message registered as read and waited for the three dots to appear beneath, indicating Robin was working on a response. He watched for a while, the movie soundtrack incongruous in the background. When the screen went dark, he watched the movie for a while, but his attention kept being pulled back to the blank phone sitting next to him on the sofa.

Finally, it buzzed.

Robin: *Honestly, I don't know. This is an entirely new thing for me. It feels huge and risky and the potential for hurt is enormous. This could be why I generally don't date. I guess I need to know there's a connection—a real one—before we go face-to-face. I need to know that when we meet, you're going to want to sit with me and talk with me—for me. With me.*

Dan: *I'm not sure I follow.*

Unless…

Dan: *Okay, however I put this, it's probably going to come out as somehow wrong or insensitive. I'll apologize in advance, and also state that if there's a right way for me to address this, please educate me. Okay? Are you…*

Sweat broke out along Dan's hairline, and the movie soundtrack now felt intrusive rather than simply odd.

...like, disabled, or... differently-abled?

The three dots indicated Robin was working on a reply, but Dan felt the need to jump in with more. *It would be okay if you were. I'm enjoying getting to know you. But if/when we do meet, you'll have to let me know if I'm...*

How to put this?

...not treating you with respect? I haven't spent a lot of time around people who navigate life differently.

Was that rude? Dan continued to sweat because he didn't know if he could make any sort of promises. It had never occurred to him that Robin might be in a wheelchair, or missing limbs, or... scarred? Maybe he suffered from a chronic condition or disease. *Like IBS, Dan?* Oh, man, he should have been kinder to Harold.

"Am I a horrible person?" he asked his empty living room.

Thankfully, his furniture did not reply that most truly awful people were 100% okay with themselves.

Dan picked up his phone, ready to type out a treatise on how open-minded he'd like to be and how willing he was to learn about anything Robin could throw at him. The screen had gone dark again. Dan woke it and saw a long message from Robin.

Robin: *Before you decide you're a horrible person who can't imagine dating anyone who doesn't fit your idea of 'dateable'—we could define this in any number of ways, but let's be kind to ourselves—let me put you at ease. No one would ever hire me to model their underwear or jeans or shirts or even paper bags. I'm not ugly enough to break a mirror, but I'm not going to win any beauty contests. I like my face, though. It's been with me for nearly fifty years, and I've grown used to it. My friends seem to like it. None of my partners have complained.*

Physically, I'm 100% functional, except for my knees. They creak alarmingly when I climb stairs. I possess two arms and legs and ten fingers and ten toes. My ears work well enough (how do you feel about subtitles?) and my eyes work well enough behind their corrective lenses. Yes, I wear glasses.

I'm average in the realm of averageness. I'm... plain.

Dan: *Who isn't? I'm not going to win any beauty contests either and have you ever seen a model without their makeup? Aliens. All of them. And there should totally be a law against celebrities appearing in public without the assistance of a stylist. Except Keanu Reeves. He's allowed to appear wherever, whenever, wearing whatever. As long as it's black. Or a very dark brown. And there's a motorcycle nearby.*

Robin: *Lol. Obsession with Keanu Reeves, check.*

Dan: *Are you shy? Is that why we're not doing this face-to-face?*

Robin: *That's a part of it. The bigger part is that I'm not sure if I'm ready.*

Breathing out slowly, Dan nodded in silent agreement. He got it… except, maybe he didn't?

Dan: *I get it. Kind of. From my own perspective, I just realized that while I've been alternately down and angry over being single again, it hasn't all been terrible. I've had a ton more time to spend with the friend I keep mentioning. Trevor. I missed him, you know? We drifted apart a little when I first got married, which I guess happens. But right when we started to get close again, he had to go away for work. To California for, like, eight months. It was right around the time I was figuring out my marriage had issues, so it came as a double blow. Losing him, then my husband. I feel like we've gotten closer again lately, though.*

The idea of Trevor moving to the West Coast poked up out of a hole like a prairie dog sniffing the air.

Dan: *I found out this week that he's in love. He's been with the guy for over a year, so it's not unexpected. I actually feel like an ass for being surprised by it. Maybe we haven't gotten as close as I imagined we had. If he moves back to CA to be with this other guy, I'll miss him, though. A lot. We get together a couple of times a month to do shit like this. Cook and watch a movie. We cook huge batches of stuff, and I freeze the leftovers to eat in between. He's super easy company. I can tell him anything. I already told him about you. And... honestly? I don't know why I'm telling you all this except to say that I think that's what I'm looking for in a relationship, you know? Someone to hang with. Talk with, cook with, curl up on the couch with. I want sex, intimacy, but it's the other stuff I need more.*

He should stop rambling.

Dan: *I guess what I'm saying is that I don't care if you're not a GQ cover model or the most interesting man in the world. Neither am I. Let's take our time. All the time you want. Let's get to know each other. I'm cool with how things are.*

Robin's reply took a long time to arrive, and when it did, Dan's gut churned all over again.

Robin: *Have you ever spent time analyzing your feelings for Trevor?*

Dan: *What do you mean?*

Robin: *Maybe you already have what you're looking for.*

Sixth Date

Dan had already scoped out the public bathroom at the Philadelphia City Hall twice, anxiously assessing every man who came and went. If he visited a third time, the security guard stationed near the entrance would notice.

He walked back toward the glass doors of the visitor's center, checking the time. His date was due in ten minutes. Maybe if Dan hadn't arrived early for all of his dates, he might have avoided the bathroom scenes—of which there'd only actually been one.

"Dan?"

The man standing in front of him was almost distressingly normal. Good-looking in a faded, approaching-fifty kind of way—jaw not quite as square as it might once have been, hair a little thin on top but still there. Dan found the liberal streaks of silver at the guy's temples comforting. So, too, the slightly creased button-down shirt and light gray slacks.

Dan extended a hand. "Sam?"

Dan and Sam. They could be a kids' storybook. Even their nearly matched, nonoffensive outfits would work. Dan's pants were dark brown, his shirt a touch crisper, but… Well, yeah.

Sam's face creased into a smile obviously meant to convey good humor. They shook.

Tucking his hand back into a pocket, Dan glanced around the bustling lobby of City Hall. "Have you been here before?"

"Nope, that's why I thought meeting here, doing the tour, could be…" Sam shrugged.

"If we don't find much to talk about, we can always pay attention to the guide."

Sam shrugged again.

Dan pulled his hands from his pockets and smoothed his palms against his thighs. "Should we buy tickets?"

Sam produced two stubs. "Already done."

"Oh. How much do I owe you?" *And have you not been stood up enough times to put off buying a ticket for your date until he actually shows up?*

"Don't worry about it."

The door to the visitor center opened, and a tall, slender woman poked her head out. "Tour starts in five minutes. We'll be meeting over there." She pointed out a spot a few feet away.

Sam shuffled his feet and shrugged. Dan searched for something to say.

"Do you have any pets?" Sam suddenly asked.

Dan blinked. "Um, no. I wouldn't mind a cat. Bookshops should have cats, I think. But I love my couch and would hate to have to choose between a cat and a couch."

"What do you mean?"

"Claws. Cats claw things. Don't they?"

"Yes. They do."

Current *Gilmore Girls* score: negative ten.

Dan cleared his throat. "How about you? Pets?"

"I have cats."

"And a couch?"

Though Dan had asked the question with his best teasing lilt, Sam responded with the same smile with which he'd greeted Dan only a few minutes prior. The one that creased his whole face but still managed to read as not quite genuine. "I'm actually on my third couch."

Dan laughed.

Sam did not.

"How many cats?" Dan asked.

"Twelve."

He hadn't meant to take a step backward, but there Dan was, the space of an extra foot between him and his date, and his date still wasn't smiling. His shoulders looked as though they were about to hitch upward again, though.

"That's a lot of cats," Dan said.

Honestly, what else could he say? Ask how many dead mice Sam found in the shower every morning? How many litter boxes he maintained? Whether the cats were neutered and spayed?

"Once you pass a certain number, it's like the others seem to magically appear."

So, not fixed, then. "You could have them—"

Sam waved his hands. "Oh, I get them all done. It's the strays, you see. They show up in the yard and fall in with the others. I should probably stop putting food outside."

Ya think?

Dan forced a smile. "You're probably the favorite house in your neighborhood."

"Eh, I wouldn't say that. I've had animal control out twice. I think next door calls them. The cats can get loud. When I think about them out there in the cold weather without a nice warm home, though." He shook his head. "I just can't. So I feed them. And keep piling up the newspapers and blankets on the back patio. I even bought a couple of cat beds."

"If you're ready to start the tour," their guide called, "we'll be heading this way."

Oh, thank God.

The tour guide pointed toward the front of the building. "We're going to duck outside for a few minutes to talk about the entryway, then we'll come back in."

The tour proved fascinating, thank Christ, because Sam said nothing for the entire ninety minutes. Next to nothing. After receiving one-word answers in response to three direct queries, Dan stopped paying attention to his date and decided to enjoy the tour instead.

He loved the view from the observation deck high up in the tower and learned a lot about Philadelphia, gaining a new appreciation for the architectural styles of Center City. Then he and Sam were back in front of the visitor's center, Dan with his hands dug deep in his pockets, Sam with his shoulders pinned to his ears.

"That was great," Dan said. "I really enjoyed it."

Sam smiled his not-smile.

"Do you want to get a coffee or something?"

"I should probably head straight home," Sam said. "The cats will need feeding."

"Oh. Okay." Dan extended his hand once more. "Well, nice meeting you."

Sam shook Dan's hand, turned, and left.

Dan fumbled his phone from his pocket and dialed Trevor, who answered on the second ring.

"I don't think I'm doing this right," Dan said.

"Doing what?"

"This dating thing."

"It's the middle of the afternoon. How could you possibly mess up a date during the daytime? Where did you go? Was it another Starbucks?"

"No. City Hall in Philly."

"What, in case you suddenly decided to get married?"

"We did the tour."

"Oh. Well, that's different. How was it?"

"The tour was great. We should do it sometime."

"Sure, I'd be up for that. The date not so much?"

"He has twelve cats, probably more. They sleep on his back patio and apparently make enough noise the neighbors complain. He had to go home to feed them. After the tour."

"Twelve cats."

"I couldn't make this shit up."

A coughing sound barked down the line.

"Are you laughing? Don't be an asshole."

"Dan, seriously, how do you meet these people? Maybe you need to redo your profile."

"Or delete it."

"Was this the guy you've been chatting with?"

Dan almost missed it—the quiet flattening of Trevor's tone. Just as quickly, he dismissed it. "No. This was Sam, whose handle was, believe it or not, CatLover69."

"That's just wrong."

"Tell me about it."

"Want to come over? I'm not doing much. I was about to throw a lasagna in the oven and kick back with a beer. We could take turns playing the new *Far Cry* if you want. It's ridiculous but fun."

Dan pictured himself on the other side of Trevor's couch, both of them leaning into the afternoon sunlight coming through the window behind. An image of Trevor's face floated to the forefront of his imagination, the easy laugh lines bracketing his mouth, the flop of blond curls across his forehead.

Robin's suggestion that he might have already found what he was looking for had rocked Dan's boat a little. But in typical Dan fashion, he'd only thought it over for a short while before stowing it. Now, recognizing that habit for what it was, Dan recalled something else: he and Trevor hadn't been hanging out as often as they used to. In fact, the last time they'd gotten together had been the night Dan downloaded the Let's Connect app under Trevor's watchful gaze.

No, not watchful. Something else had lurked in Trevor's denim-blue eyes that night. Something like restraint.

When had Trevor started guarding his expression around Dan? Had it been before Dan's marriage descended into hell, or after, when Dan couldn't take two minutes away from complaining about his ex to ask Trevor how his life was going?

Or had Trevor been guarding himself since the night Dan had had too much to drink and had confessed that he should have chosen Trevor instead? Even the vague memory of what he'd said after Trevor gently turned him down had Dan wincing. Words to the effect that it couldn't possibly work between them. They were friends. Sex would kill what they had.

What they had worked because they hadn't crossed a certain line.

Right?

"You still there?" Trevor asked.

"Yeah, sorry. Was watching where I was walking." While standing with a palm flattened against one of the fat columns in the lobby of City Hall, his forehead pressed close. So, you know, not walking at all. "Can I ask you something?"

"Sure."

"Do you remember the night you'd just got back from California, and you came over for dinner or whatever, and I was making pitchers of margaritas?"

After a beat of silence, Trevor answered, "You were convinced I'd have had a better margarita in California and wanted to sway me back to the dark side."

"I was drunk."

"Yes, you were."

"I made a fool of myself that night."

Trevor said nothing.

"Did I..." Dan licked his lips and checked his peripherals. He was alone or as alone as a man could get in a public building in the center of a lively city. "I know I kind of went off the deep end later that night and I probably said some things that…" A sigh gusted out of him. "Listen, you and Kevin. I'm really happy for you, Trev. You deserve a great guy."

More silence, then Trevor asked, "Where is this coming from?"

Someone suggesting Dan examine his feelings for his best friend. And maybe a little jealousy. Okay, a lot of jealousy. Trevor was settled. Dan was not.

"I'm not sure I know why I'm doing all of this." Dan leaned away from his post to sweep a hand through the air in front of him. Of course, the gesture would be lost on Trevor. "The dating. Why am I dating?"

"You're looking for someone to be with."

"And failing to find it. I'm pretty much at the point where I'm ready to stop trying."

"Want me to go through the app with you? I could vet some of the profiles. Two eyes are better than one and all that."

There is was again—the quiet reserve in Trevor's tone. It had to be Dan's imagination. He was projecting.

"I think I need to try something else," Dan said.

"Maybe the online thing isn't the best approach for you. Didn't you used to have a book club at Little Volume?" Trevor asked. "You could start something like that again. Book some writer-things. I've got some resources there. Come to some more lectures. You could try getting out more, you know. There's always the bar scene. Not everyone out there is young and beautiful and available for one night only. Some of us old folks are out there too. Waiting."

Except you.

Dan pressed his thumb and forefingers into his eyes, closing them, squeezing his fingers together over the bridge of his nose. He sighed into his phone. He had to get over this thing he had for Trevor. He'd done it before. He could do it again. His best friend shouldn't have to take on the burden of lonely Dan as well as sad and neurotic Dan.

"Thank you for being the best friend ever, but I think I'm gonna go home."

Trevor's reply was quiet. "Okay."

"I need to unpack some books. Cook this week's dinners. Fuck, I don't know. Get on with it, I suppose." *Could you sound less depressed?* "The book club is a good idea. I'm going to look into that."

"Sounds like a plan."

Dan grunted into the phone.

"Dan?"

"Hmm?"

"I'm always here. You know that, right?"

Voice thick with emotion he didn't understand, Dan managed a "Thanks" and ended the call.

Seventh Date

Dan: *I just figured out we never talked about my name. Were you politely ignoring my slip?*

Robin: *...yes?*

Dan: *I'm going to take that as 'I didn't notice.'*

Robin: *Guilty as charged. Where was this slip?*

Dan was in the storeroom at the back of the shop. The small room had started life as an office, back when he had more staff. Not one local student to cover the desk on weekends.

When he'd had two book clubs, entertained writers on tours, hosted a local poetry group, and done a Saturday morning story time for kids.

Studying the towers of boxes, and the wire rack shelves heaped high with more books, Dan thought back to the last time he'd been able to sit at the desk. Now stacks of remainders buried the top. Books he needed to either pack and ship or mark down for the bargain table. A mess of paper clung to one corner, a fishing tackle box full of tools he used to clean up older books open on top, covered in a fine layer of dust.

He should spend more time in here cleaning and organizing. Actually doing the work required to keep his shop in business. He loved Little Volume. Owning a bookshop had been his lifelong dream. The time to remember that was long past due.

But first, he wanted to continue his unscheduled chat with Robin.

So… the slip. Revealing his name. Did it matter whether Robin had noticed or not? It'd taken Dan this long to remember.

He set his coffee cup down and cleared off a chair. Tugged his phone out of his pocket and sat with the Sunday *Times* across his lap.

Dan: *It was days ago. Don't worry about it.*

Robin: *I went back to look and couldn't find it, so consider it forgotten.*

Dan: *Aren't you even curious?*

Robin: *I'm not sure how to answer that. I mean, if I say yes, will you ask about my name? Because I'm not ready for that.*

Dan was starting to suspect Robin would never be ready for that. Periodically, he'd checked back with Robin's profile, wondering if Robin had posted a picture or updated his connection status. Dan wasn't sure how he'd feel if Robin's status read *currently connecting*, site code for *chatting exclusively*. The code wasn't official but most users paid attention to status updates. Why put effort into connecting with someone who was "currently connecting" with someone else?

Dan had not updated his status. He didn't know what he and Robin were doing. It felt like dating, but it also did not feel like dating. He didn't think he was ready to go exclusive.

Was Robin? What did Robin want?

Dan: *Are you chatting with anyone else? This isn't a status-update kind of question. I was just curious. I've shared some of my dating horror stories with you, and I guess I wondered if you had stories to share as well.*

Of course, as soon as he'd hit send, Dan wished he could take the question back, because if Robin was talking to someone else—in the same way he spoke to Dan—it would feel weird. And Dan knew, with absolute certainty, that he had no right to that feeling. Not while he balanced his time and thoughts between Robin and Trevor.

His phone buzzed.

Robin: *I've chatted with a few people. None of them have sent me a recipe that had me calling three separate supermarkets. Yet.*

Several piles of books seemed to exhale. Or maybe that was Dan. He quickly formulated a question to steer their conversation away from deep water.

Dan: *Do you have any pets?*

Robin: *No. Why?*

Dan: *No reason. Making conversation.*

Keeping things light.

Dots danced beneath his last message. Dan set his phone on the desk next to his coffee and shook the paper out across his lap. He'd finished the first page of the comics when Robin's reply came through.

Robin: *I had a dog for a long time. When he died, I thought about getting another dog right away, but couldn't settle on one. I visited the local shelter three times. I still get these flashes of guilt when I think about the earnestness on the faces of some of those dogs. I mean, they wanted a home and I wanted to give them a home, but every time I thought about having to bond with one of them, it was like my heart slammed a door. Like, I could hear it bang shut. I'm surprised no one else could. I had suffered something of a disappointment elsewhere around the same time and was feeling emotionally bruised.*

One of the attendants there, at the shelter, I guess they'd dealt with grieving pet parents before or whatever, suggested I wait a while. It's been a couple of years now, and I haven't gone back. Thinking about going back makes me feel really tired.

Dan read over the reply a couple of times before putting the phone aside to drink some coffee—now cool and bitter, but, hey, it was still caffeinated. He took a slow sip.

Something in the way Robin described his grief resonated. The tiredness. Dan had felt that way for a long time after his divorce, and even now, a year later, a sense of extreme weariness edged in around his thoughts sometimes. Usually when he contemplated social activities. He'd felt it while reading some of the profiles on the site. At the beginning of a couple of his dates. Definitely toward the end of most.

Not when he chatted with Robin, though. Did that mean something?

Dan: *Do you think that tiredness is your body or your mind's way of telling you to slow down? That you're not ready?*

Robin: *I do. I mean, it could be a convenient excuse. Much as I miss the companionship, and his personality, his uniqueness, I don't mind not having a dependent. Or maybe it was that he was so unique that another dog wouldn't work and I instinctively know that. Imagine me shrugging. I truly don't know.*

Dan: *I get it. In a way, I think that's why I've waited so long to date. Can I share something kind of personal?*

Robin: *Maybe? If it'd be better saved for your doctor, then...*

Dan: *Ha ha. Yeah, no. It's about that tiredness. That's how I feel about this dating thing a lot of the time.*

Robin: *Meaning, you don't think you're ready?*

Dan: *I don't know. I enjoy talking with you. I've been excited about getting out there to meet some of my other connections. But sometimes, when I'm browsing a profile, I want to go lie down instead.*

Robin: *You're fifty, right? Naps are a thing. I personally enjoy a well-timed nap. Naps are, like, a modern version of ambrosia. All hail the humble nap.*

Dan: *You like naps. Got it.*

Robin: *So much so, I can feel one in my immediate future.*

Robin: *That does not mean talking to you makes me feel tired, btw.*

Dan laughed. He sent back: *I honestly didn't connect the two. Before you go, can we talk about something that *might* make you feel tired?*

Robin: *Sure? (If I go quiet, as in I don't reply right away, I got tired and went to lie down.)*

Dan: *Lol*

Dan: *After the City Hall date yesterday I got to wondering if I really was ready, and I think I am. Like, I have been disappointed by my dates so far, but I've somehow managed to connect with you. Thing is, what we're doing is easy. It's just chatting. I'm not even sure we could call last weekend a date. It was more like hanging out with a friend.*

I guess that's what I wanted to ask about. What are you looking for out of this? Is it a friend? Because if that's it, I wanted you to know I'm okay with that. I had kind of hoped that at least one of my dates would end up kicking off a friendship. That might be, I don't know, old-fashioned of me, or just plain weird. But something my grandmother told me has always stayed with me. She said always say yes to a date because even if it doesn't work out, you might make a good friend.

Of course, the bit she'd added next was what made it memorable: you never know who they might introduce you to. Trevor had introduced Dan to Chris. Taken by that measure alone, his grandmother's advice should be discarded. But Dan had always liked the first part better. He'd been a shy kid, and even at fifty, often felt awkward around new people.

Dan: *That being said, if you were interested in being friends, maybe we could meet up. No expectations. I mean, it would be nice to have plans with someone that didn't include any sort of dating agenda. Think about all the shit we could dispense with. We could hang out.*

Dan wasn't sure what the purpose of his long missive had been except for the fact he wanted to figure out what he and Robin were doing. He wanted to avoid the weariness that edged in when he wondered whether it would lead to anything useful. Could they undercut potential pain by getting right to the point?

Reading over what he'd sent, though, he wished he'd held off. What harm did it do either of them to continue chatting? But what was done was done.

Robin didn't reply for a long, long time. His bright little avatar didn't even bounce to the bottom of the message chain, indicating he'd read what Dan had sent and was at least thinking it over.

Had he wandered off and succumbed to that nap after all, or had he scanned the text as it came in and sat there thinking about it? Dan read over his message again, wincing at the rambling nature, and tried to put himself in Robin's place. Would he feel rejected by Dan's suggestion? Attacked? Dismayed?

This was why a text relationship, ultimately, wasn't going to work out. Dan spent too much time wondering about Robin's reactions—mostly because he was invested. And he had to admit, however grudgingly, that his message had been meant as a not-so-subtle push. He needed to know where this was all going.

Suddenly antsy, Dan pushed the newspaper aside and rose from the chair. He attacked the closest stack of books and quickly sorted them into three new piles. He sorted the papers next, finding more than half could be tossed into the recycling bin. When that filled, he bagged it and glanced around the office for an update on his performance.

Sadly, the room did not look much different. Dan sorted more books, pricing a few from memory and stacking them on the wheeled cart he used to stock shelves. When his phone eventually buzzed, he jumped half a foot. He snatched it up and woke the screen. It was a text from Trevor asking if he wanted to walk the Pennypack Trail, seeing as it was sunny.

It was? Dan squinted at the single high and narrow window behind the wire shelves. The glow of dusty haze suggested it could be sunny out there.

After checking the time, and the still-unread status of the message from Robin, an urgent need to return to the real world gripped him. To be with someone tangible, even if reality insisted Trevor was unobtainable. Either way, it would be a good opportunity for Dan to simply exist in his *friendship* with Trevor. To forget his longing and reconnect with the man who'd so often been there. Who'd repeatedly said he always would be there.

To be a good friend in return.

Dan sent back a yes and ventured into the store to see whether his student was happy (and alive) and able to close. Then he hopped up the back staircase to his apartment. He needed to change. And something to eat—unless they'd get something after their walk? What was the temperature out there, anyway? Dan dug out his phone to check.

Robin still hadn't read his message.

Trevor

Eighth Date

When Dan got to the park, Trevor was waiting for him, leaning against his old Subaru, peering at his phone. Though the sun shone brilliantly, Trevor wore a fleece-lined flannel hoody in a deep forest green that complimented his coloring, blue jeans, and one of his six pairs of Merrell hiking boots. Trevor would probably wear hiking boots to his wedding—which Dan would not be thinking about right now.

He looked fit and relaxed and young, which sucked. He was two years older than Dan. Close up, the paler strands at Trevor's temples would reveal themselves as silver rather than blond. If he grew a beard, it would be gray. Trevor had always had laugh lines, always the appearance of someone who enjoyed the outdoors. He never seemed to get older, though. Dan had no idea how he managed it.

"We eat the same things, get the same amount of sleep, and spend the same number of hours watching terrible movies. How is it you never look as old as me?" Dan asked by way of greeting.

Trevor glanced up. "I have good genes." He pocketed his phone. "And I don't have quite the same disappointments you have."

"What does that mean?" Dan jerked his chin toward the path. "Are we hiking up or down?" Not that a ramble along the Pennypack Trail counted as a hike, but they'd be walking for an extended period of time and Dan had worn his boots.

"Let's head north. If we get to the end, we can congratulate ourselves on a five-mile walk. If not..." Trevor shrugged.

Dan winced.

"What?"

"Sorry. Yesterday's date had a shrugging habit. It's going to be a while before I interpret a shrug as a normal, careless gesture again."

"Heh." The twist of Trevor's lips added: *only you.*

Dan made sure his shoulder connected with Trevor's as he walked past. A friendly rebuff that Trevor leaned into for a second before they hit the trail.

"You want to talk about it?" Trevor asked.

"The shrugger? No, I think I said all I needed to say yesterday."

"Have you spoken to him since?"

"No." Dan frowned into the cool sunshine, reliving the disappointment of his message to Robin having remained unread. "I can't imagine he'll message me. He didn't seem to enjoy the date, which is kinda insulting. Despite the cats and the shrugging, I thought it went okay. I mean, we didn't get much of a chance to talk. But when I invited him for coffee, he practically ran away, so—" Dan threw up his hands "—I don't fucking know. Let's talk about something else. How was your week?"

Trevor's shoulders hitched halfway upward and stopped. Dan chuckled.

Grinning boyishly—because with his curls and tan, Trevor would be forever boyish—he said, "I showed up to lecture, and students showed up to listen, and we all played our parts solidly but blandly."

"Sounds very much like my week." Dan peered skyward once more. "Nice day for March. Not as warm as it looks, though."

Trevor mock-shivered. "What is with the weather lately?"

"Are we going to spend the next hour talking about the weather?"

"You started it."

So he had. "Let's talk about something else."

They walked on in silence for about a minute before Trevor let out a soft snort. "Ever wonder if there's an upper limit on the conversation between two people and once it's reached, that's it, there's nothing new to talk about?"

"I think that's what happens in some marriages," Dan mused. "There's probably a meter for it, or an algorithm, or whatever. Like that thing about putting a penny in a jar for every time you have sex with someone before you're married, and then after you're married, you get to take one out each time."

"I thought that was only for straight people." Trevor wrinkled his nose. "So, if you do manage to take all of the pennies back out, is your marriage working?"

"I guess? Unless it takes, like, twenty years."

"What does it matter if it does? Marriage is about more than sex. It's about everything else as well."

Dan spread his hands. "That only supports your earlier theory about running out of conversation."

"How?"

"What if all you're doing at that stage is talking, and it's truly deep and meaningful stuff, but the day you take that last penny out of the jar, the conversation dries up?"

Trevor didn't answer right away. The clack of bare branches in a high breeze filled the quiet. Soft voices drifted toward them from farther along the trail.

"So, all points of connection stutter and fail at the same time?" Trevor finally said.

"Maybe. I dunno. Why were we having this conversation?"

"Because someone didn't want to talk about the weather."

Dan snorted. Gazed up at the bright sky. "Do you remember having days like this when we were kids? Warm winter days? Being able to wear a T-shirt in March?"

"It's not exactly T-shirt weather. But, if you'll remember, I grew up in California."

"And you live here why exactly?"

"Oh, a little thing called work. Also, I have this pain-in-the-ass friend who'd probably become a social hermit if I moved away."

Dan stopped walking. "Really? You think I'd hole up if you left?"

"How long was it before you went outside—willingly—after Chris?"

"Point." Dan started walking again.

After his divorce, Dan had moved into the apartment over the shop, thankful he hadn't replaced the previous tenant. The novelty of living above his place of work had yet to wear off, but Dan did sometimes wonder if he'd still be clinging to his couch more hours than not if Trevor hadn't come to his rescue.

"You know, you coming back to Pennsylvania then, with a boyfriend, probably did more to get me off the couch than you coming back alone."

Trevor stopped. He turned a quizzical expression toward Dan. "What do you mean?"

Dan wafted one hand through the air. "You were full of purpose. Otherwise, we might both still be on my couch."

With a slight bob of the head, Trevor acknowledged the point. "You ever talk to Chris?"

"No, I do not."

"You don't know what he's up to, then."

"Do you? You introduced us, remember. He was your friend."

A light flush colored Trevor's cheeks.

Dan felt his forehead crease. "What?"

"He got married last month. I thought you knew. You signed up for that dating site the same weekend."

"Because you insisted I was too young to die!"

"I thought you were depressed about the wedding, not still depressed about your divorce."

Didn't they amount to basically the same thing?

Dan sucked in air that smelled like cold concrete and wood smoke. It was a combination of scents that always invoked the sense snow might be imminent. He looked up at the clear blue sky and noted the edges, visible through the wintry tree line, had faded to a whitish gray. Their March sunshine would soon be a memory.

He turned to Trevor, who stood facing him, a quizzical crease furrowing his brow. "Can we talk about you instead? Or not talk at all?"

Trevor's lips twisted one way and then the other. He started walking again. After watching his retreating back for a few seconds—noting the stiff line of Trevor's shoulders and slightly jerky pace of his feet—Dan jogged to catch up.

He kept the silence Trevor had apparently chosen for both of them for another few seconds, before asking, "So, you and Kevin. Have you guys talked about relocating to the same coast?" See, he could be a supportive friend.

Trevor didn't answer for a while. Then he stopped walking again. Turned to face Dan and spoke so quietly, Dan wasn't sure he'd heard the words. "Kevin and I broke up."

Did he just say…? "Wait, what? When?"

Trevor huffed out a sigh. Shoved his hands into the front pocket of his hoodie. "A long time ago, Dan. About a month after I got back from California. The long-distance thing wasn't working out."

"Wait, hold up. A month after... So, like, a *year* ago?"

Dan's thoughts refused to connect, as though he held the parts from two different furniture kits and was trying to make them fit. Then the crushed gravel of the path seemed to shift beneath his feet. The sky revolved overhead, the blue center expanding and contracting. Cold gripped his shoulders as the white clouds pressed in.

Stepping off the path, Dan reached for a tree to support his suddenly shaky legs.

Trevor was not in love with Kevin. He would not be moving away.

The revelations should have been a reason for joy, but Dan couldn't get over the fact Trevor had been lying to him for a year. Couldn't understand why. Wait, did that mean—

"Was this before or after margarita night?" Dan asked.

"Before."

"What the fuck, Trev?" Trevor winced, and Dan pressed another question into the space between them. "Why did you insist I sign up for a dating site if you were—" Heat scorched Dan's cheeks. He turned his embarrassment on the tree beside him, looked past it. Shoving his hands into his pockets, he made for the path. "I think I should go."

"Dan, wait." Trevor caught Dan's arm above the elbow. "Can I say something?"

Dan jerked his arm free. "Like what?"

Trevor pushed his fingers into his hair, dragging the curls back. With his forehead exposed, his face seemed narrower—and older. His nose longer and somehow more pronounced. It took Dan a moment to connect the fact Trevor's mouth was moving with the words now hanging unheard between them. Words that were nothing but sound.

"Sorry, what?" he asked.

"You're going to be the death of me. You do realize that, don't you?"

"I have no idea what you're talking about!"

"Then listen! That night..." Dan folded his arms behind his head and squeezed his eyes shut.

"The night I made a drunken pass at my best friend and he kindly turned me down," Dan prompted. More quietly, he asked, "If you and Kevin were done, why did you say no? Do you really think—?"

An intrepid jogger passed them on the pathway, footsteps crunching in and out like a sound effect.

Dan took another step away, shaking his head. He shouldn't be asking this, because he didn't want to know the answer.

"What you're thinking is completely wrong," Trevor said. "Just so you know."

"What, that you turned me down because you don't see me that way? Or that I'm not your type and never have been? That this crush I've been nursing for years now, even when I was goddamned married, is a completely one-sided affair and I should get over it? The sooner the better. Or, maybe not, because after today, we'll likely never speak again."

Trevor's expression had morphed through several variations while Dan spoke. From pity to confusion to pain to an indecipherable combo effect.

"What?" Dan asked.

"Dan, God. I've *always* seen you that way."

The words Dan had always wanted to hear. Somewhere, in the back of his mind, he registered that fact, but not before he also logged Trevor's tone, and the return of easily recognizable pain to his old-young-how-had-I-never-noticed-how-long-his-nose-is face.

"I... don't... understand," Dan stammered.

"Because you never *listen*. You don't *look*. You're so damn self-absorbed, and you want to know the crazy thing? One crazy thing? I've always admired that about you. I thought you'd be okay after the divorce because you always put yourself first, and you'd realize you didn't need him to make you whole. You've never really needed anyone."

Dan took a step forward. "That is patently untrue." He poked a hard finger into the flannel over Trevor's chest. "I need you. You have always been the one to stand between me and the edge. Always. Without you, I'd be—"

A louder crunch than the footsteps of a single jogger pulled his attention sideways. Dan watched the family and their dog approach. Perhaps sensing the argument between Dan and Trevor, they all wore cautious expressions.

Dan stepped right off the path, back toward the trees along the river. Trevor didn't grab him again, but he did keep up, step for step, until Dan stopped again. Turned around.

Trevor stopped a short distance away, arms folded, brows drawn down.

And, God, he was beautiful in his broodiness. In his anger and resentment. Not boyish at all.

Dan shook his head toward the ground. "What have we done?" he implored his boots. "What the fuck have we been doing?"

Ninth Date

Trevor said nothing on the way back to the parking lot. Dan attempted to draw him out twice before deciding silence might serve them better. They'd rolled back the carpet to discover a trapdoor to which neither of them held the key. They just had to go find one, right? It'd be in a drawer, or a shoebox under the bed. It was probably on top of the washing machine, retrieved from a pocket years ago and dropped into the cup that held green pennies and lint.

When they'd found it, they could get together and open the door. Or, you know, talk. Figure out what was hidden beneath the floorboards. Haul each and every one of those boxes out, line them up, and start opening them one at a time.

Driving home, Dan repeated these thoughts to himself, half with the intent of setting this fantastical plan in motion, half with the thought he might actually write it all down. He'd been selling books for nearly three decades. Wasn't it time he wrote some for himself?

But even as that thought fizzled beneath the weight of the usual objections to actually writing rather than simply reading, Dan continued playing the metaphor over and over in his mind. It was damn apt. When he cast his thoughts back to the very beginnings of his friendship with Trevor, he could see the empty boxes standing around them, flaps folded back at uneven angles, waiting for their load of denial.

"I should have asked him out that very first day," he said to the steering wheel.

The steering wheel chose not to reply. It did deliver a slight shudder to his palms, though, suggesting he might need new tires. Or a wheel alignment or—

What a mess.

Dan checked for messages when he got home. Nothing from Trevor, nothing from Robin. He tossed the phone onto the table in the kitchen and went to hang from the fridge door while he peered disconsolately at shelves populated by condiments. Suspect shadows lurked inside the vegetable drawers. He shut the door and pressed his head against the stainless steel, the appliance's hum buzzing into his brain and quieting all thought for a blissful moment.

He clearly remembered meeting Trevor for the first time seven years previously. Dan had signed up for a lecture series at the university library. Trevor had been the lecturer. After the first lecture, Dan had stayed for a Q&A, and had been delighted by the invitation to join the smaller group for drinks at a nearby bar.

Lifting his head away from the fridge, Dan opened the freezer door. He tugged a package of frozen tortellini off the icy bottom shelf and tossed it on the counter. With the motley collection of vegetables wilting in the drawers, a can of crushed tomatoes, and some stock, he could put together a stew or soup that might last a few days.

The simple task of cooking set his mind free to wander again.

Before they entered the bar, Trevor had been Dan's focus. The tall, youthful literature professor was exactly the kind of guy Dan had always wanted to take home. But once they were inside, everything changed. Trevor had introduced Dan to Chris, another friend, and Chris had made it *his* mission to take Dan home.

Flattered by the attention, Dan had fallen quickly in with Chris's plans.

Up until Chris, Dan hadn't experienced romance on any scale. He'd been too shy to indulge in more than a furtive hookup in college, and once newly invested in his position as a book buyer for a large, national chain, he'd been too focused on his career to look for a relationship. His memory of those years was much like his memory of college. Random hookups in hazy settings that both exhilarated and disappointed. He'd never had a proper relationship. In fact, he'd pretty much decided he'd be better off alone, until the night he met—

If asked for an official record, Dan would finish that sentence with *Trevor*, even though Chris had been the one to take him home. And if further asked what had swayed his attention away from Trevor and toward Chris, Dan would say he didn't know.

Except, now, seven years later, standing in his kitchen, knife in hand, salted water steaming gently on the stove next to him, he'd grudgingly (or not) admit that he did.

The consideration of two men, after a long spell of disappointment, had gone to his head. Dan could have been anyone's that night. He'd gone home with Chris because Chris had asked. He'd stayed with Chris because he'd thought he was in love.

Stilling the motion of the knife, Dan closed his eyes.

He'd pursued and kept up his friendship with Trevor because he'd never gotten over the spark of attraction between them. In fact, he'd used it. Hadn't it felt good to keep them both? Forget the fact his and Trevor's friendship had transcended whatever Dan had shared with Chris.

Or was it Trevor who'd provided the emotional connection Dan had never had with his husband?

"Jesus."

Dan put the knife down. Snatched his phone from the table and called Trevor. Trevor didn't answer. Dan disconnected halfway through the invitation to leave a voice mail and brought up the text message screen instead.

Dan: *We need to talk.*

Translation—Dan needed to talk.

Dan: *Or maybe I need to. I *need* to understand how all of this happened. I've got this notion, this feeling, that Chris played us both. Is that what happened? It's not all his fault, though.*

Dan chewed on his lower lip, worrying another tiny skin fragment loose. Vaguely, toward the back of his skull, in the sliver of space not occupied by the tumult of his emotions, drifted the thought he should drink some water. Putting his phone aside, Dan filled a glass and drained it. Filled it again.

Then he grabbed his phone and thumbed furiously.

Dan: *I chose the wrong guy. I've always known I chose the wrong guy. But, Trev, why didn't you fight for me? If you've felt this way all along, why didn't you say something? What was the worst that could happen? Your friendship has meant more to me over the past seven years than anything else. You have been my constant. I'd like to think we could have built on that. That we still could.*

If their friendship survived the revelations of the day. Dan knew he played the part of self-absorbed ass to perfection, but a portion of the blame had to lie hidden in the boxes Trevor had packed and stored beneath their trapdoor. He'd let Dan go. Twice now.

Dan put the phone aside to resume cooking.

As he was setting a steaming bowl on the table, his phone buzzed. Dan snatched it up. Robin had finally replied. Heartbeat fluttering in his throat, Dan opened the message.

Robin: *Sorry it took me so long to get back to you. I had a lot of thinking to do. A part of me wanted to disappear. That seemed kind of weak, though. I didn't think you'd wonder about me for long, but I didn't want to end something I've come to enjoy without saying a proper goodbye.*

Though he'd yet to eat any of his dinner, Dan's stomach churned. He let the phone screen darken while he stared at his bowl of soup, stew, whatever, and wondered whether he had the mental fortitude to read the rest of Robin's message. Obviously, they were breaking up.

Not that they'd been together. But it almost felt as though they had. Robin had been the one bright spot in Dan's online dating experience.

Then again, letting him go would be something of a relief because for as much as Dan had enjoyed connecting with Robin, he'd been aware—on some level—that he and Robin would never meet. That Robin lacked the wherewithal to reach across…

An icy finger skated down Dan's spine.

No.

No!

He'd already decided Trevor would not do that to him.

He *wouldn't.*

Trevor was his *friend.*

Dan woke the phone and scrolled back to the beginning of his conversation with Robin and read all of it over with Trevor's voice in mind. Trevor's love of metaphor, his literacy, his obstinacy, his fear of true connection. The converse ability to live a fantasy realistically enough to fool everyone.

Pushing his chair back from the table, Dan extended his legs and leaned back. He sighed out a dull and weary breath. Then the sense of loss caught him—deeply and keenly, a fine-edged blade that was only felt after it lifted away, exposing the wound to the air.

The pain wasn't for the cut, though. Or even the knife. It was the part that came from knowing he'd lost something precious, something he'd never regain. And for the futile thought that it hadn't been his fault. He'd been in love with an illusion.

No wonder his marriage hadn't lasted.

An irrational impulse slid his phone into his hand once more, fingers dialing an almost forgotten number.

His ex-husband answered on the second ring. "Dan?"

"Chris."

"To what do I owe the pleasure?"

"I, ah, heard you got married. Figured I'd wish you well and all that."

"Bullshit."

Dan said nothing.

"Why are you really calling?" Chris asked.

Dan swallowed, sure the awkward sound carried through the phone. "That night at the bar. The night we met. Did you know that Trevor, that he…?"

Chris hesitated long enough for his answer not to matter. He gave it anyway, a quiet "Yes."

"Then why?"

"What I don't get is why you two aren't together yet. I figured it'd happen as soon as I got out of the way."

"Yeah, well, life seems intent on keeping us apart." A flush heated Dan's cheeks. Had he just admitted…? Yes, he had.

"Listen," Chris said, his tone more somber. "I did want you for myself. That was always true. It wasn't always about having something Trevor didn't."

"Does he know that?"

"We don't talk much anymore. He never forgave me for divorcing you."

"I divorced you."

"Whatever lets you sleep at night."

"Chris, you were sleeping with other men in our bed."

"You were in love with someone else."

Point.

"Why is this all such a mess?" Dan asked.

"Honestly? I have no idea. If I could do it all over… I'd still take you home that night. But then that would be it. I would have let Trevor have you."

Dan's blood boiled. "Oh, that's great. Thank you so much for thinking you'd have had any control over who or what… Fuck you, Chris. Just fuck you."

Spit flew from his mouth, but Chris probably heard neither that nor the sputtering of curses that followed. He'd disconnected. Dan dropped the phone onto the table and folded his arms. Rested his head. Stared morosely into the dark space between the table and his lap. After another minute, he acknowledged he was too worked up to think clearly.

He ate a little soup, ladled the rest into freezer bags, and started getting ready for bed. Before retiring for the night, he padded back into the kitchen to connect his phone to the wall charger. The screen brightened.

Trevor hadn't texted him back, but Robin's message was still open. Dan scrolled down to the bottom and resumed reading.

Robin: *But I don't want to say goodbye. Let's do it. Let's pierce the veil. You've shared so much with me, including your name. I want to share more with you.*

Breath caught in the back of Dan's throat, nearly choking him. He put his thumb over the next part of the message, unsure if he wanted to keep reading. The vague thought that Robin might be Trevor in disguise still tickled his brain—his emotional center. Their relationship was fractured enough.

He moved his thumb.

Robin: *My real name is actually Robin. I know. I KNOW. Who'd figure out the double blind? I've always both liked and disliked it. Robins are wonderful birds, but they're so little. Robin Hood is... Well, I could write an essay about Robin Hood. Essays have been written. Films made. Too many films. The Robin I like best, though, is the most famous sidekick in history. I mean, who wouldn't want to work alongside Batman? You get to do all the things, but you're not the one who's ultimately responsible for any of it. Also, Batman.*

Despite the leftover misery spiking his gut, the weight of weariness delivered by the day, Dan grinned. The stretch of his lips felt odd, as though his skin had been glued and left to dry. He moved his mouth around a little to loosen the effect, and read on.

Robin: *Back to reality—I've enjoyed talking with you. I know I already said that, but it bears repeating because this online dating experience has not gone how I expected it to. You're the only person I'm still chatting with. No one else is interested in a little bird, or someone who's too shy to connect in person. No one else has sent me a grocery list.*

You took a chance. Now I'm going to take one. I'm going to add a photo. Tomorrow. I need to wash my hair first. (Yes, I have hair.) Then I'm going to try for a good night's sleep. I'll check to see if we're still connected when I wake up, but even if we're not, I'm going to upload a photo anyway. Even if you're not around to see it. Know it will be for you, though.

Well, fuck.

Fuck!

Dan read the note again, in its entirety, then a third time. By the fourth read, he still hadn't figured out how he felt. Giddy, in some sense, but also as though he stood at the edge of a precipice. Robin was, unequivocally, not Trevor. For one thing, their ages didn't match up.

Unless Trevor had fudged that on the profile.

Maybe tomorrow's big reveal would be his way of coming clean.

No, the whole name thing pointed in another direction. A strong direction. A highway sign, newly erected with crisp white lettering and a big fat arrow pointing that way.

Once more, Dan couldn't sort his feelings. Couldn't make sense of any of them, except the dizzy sensation of overlooking a deep, dark hole (the promise of Robin's photo notwithstanding).

There was only one thing to do.

He put the phone down and went to bed.

Tenth Date

Snow blanketed the world the next morning, a thick white carpet that mocked the sunshine of the day before. In no hurry to open Little Volume, Dan wallowed in bed while the snatches of sleep he fell into became shorter than the time he spent lying awake and thinking. His back started to ache from doing nothing.

A faint pounding finally roused him. After figuring out the sound was coming from the door at the bottom of the stairs rather than the blood pushing sluggishly toward his heart, Dan pulled himself out of bed. He nearly fell down the stairs to the back of the shop. He'd managed to get his robe over one shoulder by the time he opened the door. He'd lost a slipper somewhere along the way.

Dan blinked sleepily at his visitor, a young man with more freckles than face and shockingly red hair tucked under a woolly Flyers hat. He was rocking side to side, blowing on his hands. Behind him, a pickup with a plow attachment idled in the alleyway, the exhaust pipe coughing steam.

"Thirty to plow the lot," the young man said, without preamble.

Dan opened and closed his mouth a couple of times, the smack of his dry tongue somehow audible over the rumbling of the pickup. Then he inspected the snow at his feet and noticed that it reached over the bottom step. It wouldn't melt by the end of the day. It would only get heavier.

Dan offered a vague nod and gestured back toward the stairs. "Need to get my wallet."

"Sure."

Weariness settled over Dan's shoulders as he remounted the stairs, collecting his slipper along the way. He'd hoped it would be Trevor at the door. For an instant, he'd even wondered whether the red-headed stranger might be Robin—setting aside the matter of Robin finding his actual address and plucking up the courage to venture out into the real world.

Dan ignored his phone to pick up his wallet and flip through the bills inside. He pulled out enough to pay the plow guy and trundled back downstairs. The pickup swept past him, piling the last of the snow against the wall, and the driver hopped out. The young man looked from the meager collection of bills to Dan and back again.

"That was quick," Dan said out loud to emphasize the fact thirty dollars was outstanding compensation for five minutes' work.

The money disappeared. Seconds later, the truck huffed back into the alley, only to stop two doors down, behind the sewing repair shop. Dan shut and locked his door, but didn't immediately climb the stairs. He should peer out the front of the shop, see if the sidewalk needed clearing. Check if anyone else had opened.

He wanted to go back to bed.

His phone was upstairs.

Rousing himself for the second time that morning, Dan padded through the quiet dark of the shop and peered out the front windows. He would have to shovel the walk. The café across the street was open and doing a brisk business by all appearances. A number of other windows remained dark. Dan checked the time. A whisker after eight.

How was it not midday yet? He usually opened the shop around ten, so…

"Not going back to bed," he mumbled as he returned to the stairs.

In the kitchen, he snatched his phone from the charger and went back to bed. And lay there, supine, warm phone pressed to his chest.

Did twenty-first-century cellphones emit enough radiation to incite a cancerous revolt in his heart?

No, Dan. That pain has another name. One that starts with a T.

Lying there, Dan played a game called *Should I look for a message from Trevor first, or check out Robin's profile?* The pros and cons for either action unfurled side by side in his mental space, proverbial angels and devils, ready to perch on his shoulders. If Trevor hadn't answered, the choice would be simple. Look at Robin's profile. If Robin had yet to post a picture, Dan could ignore the issue for the rest of the day. He'd been ignoring the issue of Trevor for years, already.

For the first time since his divorce, Dan felt sorry for Chris. Not the combination of pity and remorse Chris probably deserved—he'd been the one to cheat, after all. More a sense of loss. He'd loved Chris. The legalization of same-sex marriage probably hadn't been the best excuse for making it official, but they'd been living together for two years by then. At the time, getting married had seemed logical.

Another morning spent in postmortem for a corpse that was beyond dead wouldn't solve his current dilemma, however. Dan lifted his phone and woke the screen.

Trevor had answered his text. A new notification also hovered over the Let's Connect app. Probably Robin updating his profile.

Decisions, decisions.

He chose Robin and opened the app. There were no new messages, but Robin's profile had been updated. Dan tapped the notification and fought the urge to close his eyes. It didn't matter what Robin looked like. It really didn't. Unless he looked like Trevor, in which case—

Breath caught in Dan's throat as the picture appeared on the little screen, too small for proper appreciation, but large enough for a passing judgment.

Robin had a nice face. Soft brown hair sprinkled liberally with gray, a short beard—also gray—nose on the large side, lips kinda thin. Possibly that was the beard. His eyes were his best feature, even behind his glasses. Large and brown, they spoke of wit, intelligence, and gentle humor. Robin's eyes also communicated the shyness Dan expected. A slight tension evident at the corners. Faint frown lines overhead.

But it was a nice face. A face Dan could definitely warm to, especially when paired with the conversation of the past couple of weeks. With that wit, intelligence, and humor.

Dan searched his phone for a picture of Trevor. He had several, and he paged through thumbnails until he found the one he wanted. Last summer, the two of them on the boardwalk at Wildwood, a place they'd simultaneously abhorred and adored. They'd gone on a dare, figuring they'd hate every minute and could reward themselves with something classy afterward. Dinner in Cape May, somewhere stuffed with nineteenth-century charm or perhaps a view of the sun as it set over the water.

Instead, they'd pursued night along the boardwalk, hemorrhaging money all over the carnival games, stuffing themselves with funnel cake, soft serve, hot dogs, and snow cones. They'd stayed through a random display of fireworks and talked about sleeping on the beach. Thank Christ they hadn't. A night on hard, packed sand would have killed their backs.

The picture captured Trevor in the golden light of late afternoon. As always, he looked ten years younger, but it wasn't so much the lack of lines or the brightness of his hair—it was his expression. Trevor looked alive. He looked happy. He was having a great day… and he cared a great deal about the person taking the photo. It was right there, in his eyes.

It was always there. Or had been, until recently.

The lurch in Dan's midsection, the knock at his heart, the burn behind his eyes—he'd felt none of these studying Robin's pic. Robin had a nice face. A good face.

He didn't have Trevor's face.

Dan knew what he had to do, and the sucky part wasn't that he'd have to get out of bed and put on real clothes. The worst part of today wouldn't be shunting a perfectly nice man permanently into the friend zone—though that would hurt. Dan liked Robin a lot and, if not for the existence of Trevor, could imagine pursuing something deeper with him. But Trevor did exist. Trevor had texted him—*we should talk*—and Dan knew he'd never move ahead until he confronted that existence—crawled to the edge of the precipice and shouted into the void beyond. Spilled his heart, all of his secrets.

Declared himself.

Then he'd crawl another few steps until all of him hung suspended over nothingness and wait either to fall or for Trevor to catch him.

Only then, only after all of that, could Dan move on.

Eleventh Date

Dan shivered on Trevor's front porch for several minutes without knocking, hoping Trevor would accidentally discover him there and… What? Invite him in or send him packing? Either would take the decision out of Dan's hands, and that, he realized, was what he wanted most. Not to have to make a choice—even though he'd already made one by coming here.

He thought about the phone in his pocket, about Robin's profile update. It wasn't too late to make a start there, or continue what they were building. But as his gaze focused again on Trevor's front door—the smoked-glass panel in the center—he recalled the day he and Trevor had bought the door.

Neither of them was particularly handy, but they'd figured the task of taking one door down and putting up another fell well within their grasp. If they'd bothered measuring anything first, they'd have saved themselves a lot of time—and several trips to the hardware store for the wood to build a new frame, more wood for a second frame, more hardware, and finally the name of a local contractor to finish the job. Or, you know, take care of the whole thing.

A weary smile tugged at Dan's mouth as he remembered Trevor's consternation over having to spend the night in a house with no door. Then he blinked as a shadow moved behind the glass and the door whispered open to reveal Trevor looking rather rumpled in old sweats and a baggy sweater. His hair poked out every which way and, for once, he didn't look younger than his years.

Without speaking, Trevor turned and disappeared inside his house. He left the door open. Dan followed, closed the door behind him, and aimed for the kitchen. Sure enough, Trevor was there, sitting stiff-backed at the small breakfast table. Tentatively, Dan pulled out the chair opposite and sat on the edge of the seat.

He swallowed. Licked his lips. Then reached deep inside, knowing he had only one chance to make this right.

"So."

Good start, Dan.

Dan put his hands on the table. Began a study of the wrinkles around his knuckles. "I'm going to start by saying I'm sorry. I…" He peeked up at Trevor, who seemed to be staring through him. "We've wasted so much time, and what I don't understand is why? I'm just a man, okay? I'm weak, full of holes, selfish—yes. I've used you badly, I know that. Keeping you as my friend. I can't say I regret the years we've spent building this, though. I've never had a friend like you, and I think…" Though the passage of actual thought through his head felt chaotic, some clarity began straightening certain lines. "I think in some way, that's what stopped me from being more honest about the way I felt. Except for when I was drunk. I've always been afraid of, well, this."

Trevor's expression had barely changed, but at that his mouth twisted. He glanced off to the side, then down at his own hands, or the fold of arms he'd tucked them into.

"Trevor, please. You need to say something."

Trevor's shoulders drooped and he shook his head. "I don't know what to say." He finally looked up. "Since yesterday, I've had no words. I…" He sucked in a breath and exhaled forcefully. Untucked his hands. "Except, fuck, Dan."

"'Fuck, Dan'?"

"You're the one who always does the talking. I answer. Give me something to work with here."

"Oh, no. You're not getting off that easy." Dan felt his brow crunch downward. "Okay, fine. Why did you put me off that night? Margarita night?"

"Seriously? You were, like, two months divorced. I hadn't been hanging around on the sidelines for six years to be a rebound."

"That's…" Fair. Totally fair. Except… "How could you be a rebound when it's always been you?"

Trevor shook his head. "Nope. You can't put that on me. You're the one who was married."

"Okay, then why did you lie about Kevin? For an entire year?"

Trevor wilted, his shoulders dropping again. "It was easier that way."

"Why?"

"Because if you'd known I was single, you'd have made another pass."

"What makes you so sure of that, and why was I the one making all the passes? You knew how I felt!" Dan's breath came quick and fast. He held his next breath in his lungs for a moment before letting it out, hoping to slow the beat of his heart. When that didn't work, he massaged his chest. Then, putting both hands back on the table, as though to brace himself, he asked, "Have I been reading this all wrong?" *Oh, God.* "Have I… Jesus. Trevor, this isn't all in my head, is it? That I want you, that you want me. That we've somehow managed to not do anything about what feels like could be everything, for six, no, seven years? It's not just me, is it?"

Trevor shook his head wearily. "No, it's not just you."

"Then why are we in such a mess?"

Trevor got up, circled the kitchen island, kicked at the fridge—which stopped growling—and landed back in his chair. He chewed his lip, crossed his legs, folded his arms, then undid every knot, letting his limbs fall easy. It was a defeated posture, and Dan feared the words that would eventually come. But he waited Trevor out, because it was Trevor's turn, damn it.

Finally, Trevor answered. "Because I was never sure I could make you glow the way he did. Chris. He was so damn smooth. I watched him sweep you off your feet like you were a goddamned Disney princess, and I knew I could never measure up. And now? With you being broken and me being me? Shit."

Instead of doing the sensible thing and pausing to process Trevor's words, Dan immediately pushed back with, "When was the last time you were actually with someone? The last time you took a risk? Because that's what it is, Trev. This." Dan pointed between them. "No promises, no guarantees. You didn't think I went into it all with Chris thinking he'd love me forever? Questioning whether that was even something I should want? I figured I'd give it a shot because all I've ever wanted is to find one person I could be myself with. And then be with that person forever."

"Could you be yourself with Chris?" Trevor challenged.

Dan snorted out a short, sad laugh. "Sometimes." He tried and succeeded in catching Trevor's gaze. "You know who I'm always myself with?"

Closing his eyes, Trevor bobbed his head.

"Do you want this?" Dan asked quietly.

"Do you?"

"Nuh-uh. You first. You know where I stand. I'm here, in your kitchen, making an ass of myself." He'd just answered the damn question, hadn't he? "What do *you* want?"

For a second, he thought Trevor might leap up again, circle the kitchen, and give the fridge another kick. For another second, it looked as though Trevor might melt, instead. Slide into a loose-limbed puddle on the floor. Then, finally, breathing in deeply and holding it there—much as Dan had done, and Dan could feel the same breath beating in his lungs—Trevor answered.

"I want to go back seven years to the night I met you. To not introduce you to Chris. To not even take you to that bar. To not have to watch you fall in love with another man, marry him, divorce him, and spend a year being sad. I want to be the one who made the first move. I want to have been the brave one. For us not to be sitting here now, all these years later, looking at a sea of eggshells so well and truly smashed, they're a fucking carpet. They're sand. Goddamn sand."

"Then let's lie on them and pretend it's a beach. That the sun is warm overhead and the ocean is sighing at our feet. We're holding hands and we're daydreaming. What we'll do in the morning, what we'll do at night. We're together and all we can think about is being together. All day, every day."

"We have jobs."

"I'm being meta-fucking-phorical!"

Trevor cracked a smile. "I know."

Dan extended a hand, pushing his fingers across the table. "Come to the beach with me."

Trevor lifted one hand and pushed his fingers across the table, stopping short. Then, with the expression of a runner crossing the finish line of the New York Marathon, he touched his fingertips to Dan's. Trevor's entire face seemed to contract then, lips trembling, skin blanching.

Dan held in the observation that it shouldn't be this hard, because his stomach had collapsed into a black hole and his whole self would end up down there if he didn't move. He nudged his fingers forward until they threaded with Trevor's.

Your move, buddy. Your move.

Trevor lifted their hands and their palms met, fingers folding together. Dan bit back a gasp. The kinetic energy snapping between them could light up a star. Could Trevor feel it?

Dan met Trevor's gaze and saw the light in his eyes, the constrained power of what Dan could feel coursing up his arm and over to the center of his chest. His stomach seemed to cave in at the same time, and for a second, the universe did collapse. He and Trevor sat in a blind, timeless, weightless moment. Then everything snapped back into place and they were sitting at Trevor's breakfast table, one hand joined, one hand each pressed to their stomachs.

"Black hole?" Dan asked.

"Did you know the Greeks used to think the stomach was where emotions were stored and felt?"

"That… explains a lot."

Trevor smiled.

"Can we kiss now," Dan asked, "or do you think sitting palm to palm is our limit for today? This is pretty heavy."

Smile stretching toward a laugh, Trevor tugged Dan's hand. "C'mere."

Dan shuffled around the edge of the table to stand in front of Trevor. Trevor caught his hip and pulled him closer. Then, with some adjusting of legs and bodies, Dan was balanced across Trevor's thighs.

"I'm afraid we're either going to break this chair or our hips, or both," Dan said.

Trevor was laughing again. "I've still got that contractor's phone number."

"You're suggesting a threesome already?"

Trevor's arms closed around Dan's back. "God, no. Not my thing."

"Good." Dan touched the tip of his nose to Trevor's. Breathed across Trevor's lips… there, so close, yet so… not far, but somehow far. As though the inch still between them might take years to cross.

Trevor took the journey, lifting his chin, touching his mouth to Dan's. His lips were cool and dry. Their bottom lips stuck together. It was awkward. It was perfect. Dan leaned in and they kissed again, softly, lips tacky and unsure. And then Dan's senses were filled with coffee and… strawberry jam. Lips that were warmer now, softer, more confident. A tongue, the touch of which did strange things to Dan's insides, as though Trevor were plugged into an outlet and delivering power.

He groaned and felt the sound returned: Trevor's lips moving and reverberating beneath his. Dan couldn't get enough, couldn't get as close as he wanted, couldn't find Trevor's skin beneath his bulky sweater, couldn't find the off button or the on button, or the way forward or back. He was lost and didn't care if he was ever found. Fuck the bookshop, fuck the university. Fuck the sunshine and their private little beach. Fuck everything.

Because right here, right now, in this one transcendent moment, lips moving in time with Trevor's, Dan had everything he'd ever wanted.

The world shifted and swayed as Trevor rose from the chair, taking Dan with him, lifting Dan out of his lap and steadying him on the floor. Breaking the kiss, Trevor grabbed Dan's hand and tugged him out of the kitchen.

"On our first date?" Dan gasped as the carpet running down the short hallway leading toward Trevor's bedroom whispered beneath his feet.

"I'm not waiting another minute," Trevor said. He pulled Dan into his bedroom, turned him around, and pushed him onto the bed.

Dan scooted backward, and Trevor crawled after him, knees straddling Dan's hips. He dipped down to kiss Dan again, and Dan decided to simply let go, to become one with the mattress. To let Trevor guide them. He'd been the one to come to the door, to get them this far. He was totally on board with whatever happened next. It was Trevor's turn.

Trevor knew exactly what he wanted.

He had Dan undressed and moaning in minutes, his hands and lips carving trails across Dan's body—heedless of the rough skin at Dan's elbows and knees, the wrinkles in odd places. The gray creeping into his chest hair and pubes. The slackness of a belly that used to be smoother, tighter.

Trevor, of course, was beautiful, but also older than Dan remembered. Always fitter, his pecs had definition. His blond chest hair still glowed like fine-spun gold. He was long and lean, all over. Freckled. Dan asserted himself for the space of time he needed to trace the pattern of freckles across Trevor's chest.

They kissed tirelessly. Stroked and pulled. Brought their hard cocks together for a rushed and heady climax—only the first, Dan suspected, and best gotten out of the way quickly. Then Trevor let Dan roll him backward and climb on top, drop kisses along a collarbone, tease one nipple to a pebbled point, then the other. To skate his tongue down the center of Trevor's torso, tasting sleep and soap and sweat. Spent semen. The bitter and salty essence of Trevor. His secret self. He took Trevor's recovered erection into his mouth and sucked, tongued, and swallowed.

Brought his lover to a shuddering climax.

Enjoyed the same from Trevor's mouth and hands.

And for all those moments, each of which seemed to pass in a second and an hour, his only coherent thought was that what they were doing was right. That this, whatever it was, would work.

After his second climax, Dan flopped onto his back and reached one arm overhead for a pillow, which he dragged down to where they were. He tugged it beneath his head. Sighed out an almighty breath.

Beside him, Trevor rumbled something like, "Mmm."

Dan closed his eyes and *reveled.* When had he last come twice in the space of a morning?

The bed dipped beside him and an arm stole across Dan's chest, warm, slightly tacky with sweat. A damp cock nudged his hip. Thankfully, not hard—but plump. Apparently not done.

"I haven't eaten breakfast yet," Dan mused quietly.

"So, what, you figured you'd come over here, sort out seven years' worth of misplaced lust, and then demand I feed you?"

Dan rolled his head in Trevor's direction, opening his eyes. "Something like that."

Trevor nudged close enough to touch their lips together. "Cad."

Dan laughed. "You say the sweetest things."

"You opening the shop today?"

"What time is it?"

"About then."

"Probably not. I don't know. I should." Dan pressed another kiss to Trevor's mouth. "I want to stay here with you. In fact, this is all I want to do for the rest of my life."

A wrinkle appeared between Trevor's eyebrows.

"What?" Dan asked. He'd lift a hand, smooth the wrinkle away, but his arms were numb.

"You know it's not always going to be this easy."

"You thought today was easy?" Dan offered a sardonic tilt of his lips that should communicate he understood Trevor's meaning.

Trevor matched the sideways smile.

"I think this is a pretty good start, though, don't you?" Dan said. "I mean, the sex could have been mediocre."

"You didn't think—"

Dan forced one of his arms to move and fastened a hand over Trevor's mouth. Trevor licked his palm.

"Quit it," Dan said. He lifted his hand.

Trevor was smiling. Then a sober expression stole across his face. "I've loved you for so long, I don't know what it'd be like not to love you."

A sudden burn shot behind Dan's eyes, centering in the middle of his face. He blinked. As though viewed through thick glass, the world expanded and contracted. And he remembered the conversation he'd had with Trevor only a week before. When he'd thought Trevor was in love with Kevin. When Dan had thought Trevor might move to the West Coast.

Trevor had told him then that he loved him, and Dan hadn't been listening. Then again, Trevor hadn't exactly been playing fair, had he?

Dan blinked. Warmth spilled across his cheeks. "These aren't tears," he said. "I'm hungry. And tired."

Trevor touched his cheek.

"What?" Dan pushed out.

"Tell me you love me."

"You don't think I do?" Dan searched Trevor's eyes, seeing things he'd never noticed before. The blue, of course, like new denim, but also flecks of gold and brown. How the color darkened toward the irises and paled slightly at the outer edge. The tiny reflection of himself in the darkness of Trevor's pupils. "I'm still mad at you," he whispered. "For letting so much time pass."

"I know."

"And I'm scared about what comes next."

"Me too."

"But if all I need to do to make this right is love you, then…" He swallowed. "We'll be okay, right?"

"You think?"

Dan's mouth crooked up on one side. "No. But it's a nice thought, isn't it? I do love you, by the way. In case that wasn't completely clear."

Trevor nodded. Squeezed Dan's fingers. "Dan, I… I'm sorry. I wish..."

Dan blubbed once, the sound embarrassing, but all he could find. Then his cheeks were warm and wet again and Trevor was in his arms, kissing his face, holding him close. He might have been crying too. Neither of them was alone in this, even though they had been for way too many years.

But now they were together. Joined all the way down. Sticky from their desire. Kissing away each other's tears and murmuring promises they intended to keep. And that was all one could ask for. All love needed to be.

Last Date

It was amazing how well one might think they knew another person—only to realize they didn't know them at all. At precisely 3:01 p.m. on Monday afternoon, Dan learned that Trevor was somewhat obsessive about laundry.

"Neither of us has showered today and we had sex, like, three times. If I don't wash these sheets now, I'll have to burn them." Trevor tugged at the pillow squashed comfortably beneath Dan's head.

"Okay, okay." Dan didn't move. Didn't want to move. Trevor's bed was a warm and cozy haven from the real world. "But I would like to state for the record, that three times is amazing. I mean—"

"Can you state that on the couch or something?"

"Why so grumpy?"

Trevor frowned at that, then checked the time on the digital display beside the bed. "I need to eat."

"You're cute when you're hangry."

Making a sound like a genuine harrumph, Trevor tugged at the pillow again. Dan relented, lifting his head. Though slightly muzzy from sleep, a sense of peace flowed softly around him—like the quilt Trevor was stripping off of his legs.

Sighing, Dan sat up and reached for his pants. His phone slipped out of one of the pockets and the cozy bubble surrounding him evaporated with a pop. He'd forgotten to message Robin.

Trevor tugged up the bottom sheet, spilling Dan off the bed, and bundled the linens into his arms. “Towels are in the closet if you want a shower,” he said.

“Is that a hint?”

With a shrug, Trevor left the bedroom.

Dan picked up his phone. Then decided he couldn’t do this naked and smelling of sex. He located a clean towel and took what he intended to be a quick shower. But once inside the tiled stall in Trevor’s bathroom, that sense of not really knowing another person swirled up again, buoyed by the scent of Trevor’s soap, which was shockingly unfamiliar. How could he not know what Trevor smelled like? And what was this? Dan poked through the bottles and bottles of different shampoos and conditioners lined along the shelf like spectators. Only one man lived here, right?

He chuckled at the razor clogged with pubes, amused at the thought of Trevor grooming, then became slightly… no, more than slightly jealous over *who* Trevor might be grooming for.

Did Trevor regularly slake his lust with other men? Was that why there were so many brands of shampoo in the shower? Overnight guests… Oh, God. That was why he wanted to wash the sheets so quickly, wasn’t it?

Dan popped out of the shower like the cork from a champagne bottle and bumped into Trevor on the mat.

“Whoa.” Trevor steadied them both before they surfed across the bathroom floor. “Where’s the fire?”

“Nowhere. Sorry. Just need to get dry.”

“You still have suds in your hair.”

“I do?” Dan looked upward, and a clump of shampoo dropped into his eye. “Ow.”

Trevor hustled him back into the shower, squashing in after him, and turned the water back on. As soon as the spray hit the top of Dan’s head, the scent of apples rose up, green and piquant.

"Good choice," Trevor said as he massaged the soap away with strong fingers. "I like following this one up with the greet tea conditioner. They smell great together. My second favorite combo is the strawberry-kiwi. The first time I used it, I kept smelling it all day, and thinking I'd left a Snapple open somewhere." Trevor picked up a dark green bottle. "This one is the best, though. It's not sweet. It's actually kind of astringent." He popped the cap, and the scent of melaleuca bark and birch all but singed Dan's nostril hairs. "Really wakes you up."

"Who are you?"

"Trevor Duvall Mackey."

"And all of these are yours?" Dan asked.

"Yep. But you already knew I was weird."

Yes. Yes, he did.

Showered, dried, and dressed, Dan felt another nap coming on, but quickly realized his weariness was more attached to the fact he'd yet to message Robin than any activity over the past half hour. He retrieved his phone from his pocket and held it up.

"I have to take care of something."

Trevor's eyebrows twitched together.

Dan licked his lips. "Robin. The guy I've been chatting with? He uploaded his picture for me last night."

"Oh." Such a small word. Short, but soft. Heavy with meaning. Trevor scratched his chin. Ducked his head. "I'll, um, go see what's in the kitchen. If… Did you want to…?" One hand flailed weakly upward.

Dan put a hand to the side of Trevor's face, the bristle of Trevor's 3:37 p.m. shadow tickling his palm. "I want to. But I need to take care of this. I… This is your fault, if you think about it."

"How so?"

"You're the one who said I needed to start dating again."

"Oh, that." Trevor winced.

"What?"

"I, er…" Trevor put his hand over Dan's, almost cuddling it to his cheek. "I had a plan, one very dark and twisted, and when I think about it now, it's so stupid. Like, what the fuck?"

Dan arched his eyebrows.

Trevor moved Dan's hand away from his face to kiss the palm, then squeezed the fingers. "So, um, it went something like this. You'd sign up, and then I'd sign up and start messaging you."

That cold finger was back; no, two of them. Pinching their way down Dan's spine. "Tell me it's not you. That Robin isn't—"

"What? No. I chickened out."

"Oh, thank God."

"No. Dan… No. The more I thought about it, the more the whole thing sounded like a bad rom com, so I sat there and listened to you prattle on about Robin instead, and it was fucking torture."

"You know, you could have come clean about the Kevin thing."

"I wasn't sure you were still interested. Also, the stuff we talked about on Margarita night, our reasons for not doing *this*… they all hold true, Dan. Your friendship—"

Dan cut him off with a kiss before whispering against his lips. "Too late. We're in deep and the only way out now is to keep swimming." He patted Trevor on the butt. "Now go find food and give me the privacy I need to let Robin down."

"You're not going to break his heart are you?"

Dan frowned down at his phone. "I don't think so. But… I'm going to hurt him and it sucks." He glanced up. "In a way, this is going to hurt me too. I liked him, Trevor. No, I do like him. He's a sweet guy."

"I feel terrible."

"You should." Dan pointed toward the door. "Food. Go."

Perching his butt on the edge of the stripped bed, Dan woke his phone and opened Let's Connect. And then sat there wondering if he could disappear. Delete his profile and *poof*!

No. Absolutely not. Even if Robin wouldn't exactly be devastated by the move—would probably recover—it was a shitty thing to do to a friend, and whether or not something had ever developed between them, Robin was that. A friend.

Dan opened the chat window, wiggled his thumbs, and started typing.

Dan: *So, guess what? You look like you. I honestly didn't have a complete mental picture, not a physical one, anyway. But your photo totally matched who I thought I was talking to. I'm going to say that's a win. I'm also going to say that I get being shy. Honestly, I do. But this picture is going to make a huge difference to your profile. I bet you've already had a bunch of new connection requests.*

It was obvious from his tone where he was going with this, wasn't it?

To Dan's shock and surprise, three dots appeared beneath his message. Oh shit.

Robin: *Uploading an actual picture of myself turned out to be a very low-key event. I spent all night tossing and turning, and then I posted it and the world didn't explode. Funny about that. And, yes, I did get new connection requests today. Guess I'm not paper bag material after all.*

Dan: *You honestly thought you were?*

Robin: *No. Not really. It's just... It's real now. Me being on here. Looking for a connection.*

Dan: *There is that.*

Seconds ticked by with neither of them adding to the conversation, and Dan knew it was up to him to say something. He was the one pulling the plug, after all.

Three dots appeared beneath his last. Blowing out a breath, Dan sat back and waited.

Robin: *I'm still not ready to do the in-person thing. I know that's... <insert your favorite curse word here>. I suck, I know. You've been super patient with me and I'm letting you down.*

Dan: *You're not. I have something to confess.*

Robin: *You're actually an alien wearing a human skin?*

Dan: *Maybe? I mean...*

Dan shook off the urge to digress, to wander aimlessly away from what he needed to say.

Dan: *I sort of had it out with Trevor yesterday. And by 'had it out,' I asked him why we weren't together. Oh, I forgot to mention the part where he admitted he was actually single and had been for, like, a year. Nearly a year. Anyway, we embarrassed ourselves in Pennypack Park, arguing about shit and walked back to our cars in the sort of silence that has weight.*

Then today we...

While Dan thought about how to break the news—not by telling Robin he and Trevor had thoroughly messed up the sheets on Trevor's bed—Robin started typing.

Robin: *It's okay. I know that's rich, coming from me. But it's okay. You don't need to be sorry or think you're breaking me into pieces or something. That sounds wrong, but you're a nice guy. You're decent. You've been pretty honest with me, and I haven't been as honest with you. I mean, I have, but I've made it hard and I don't blame you or hate you for going after something you've always wanted.*

Dan: *I feel like I led you on unfairly.*

Robin: *You did and you didn't. I knew Trevor was in the picture just about the whole time. He's what made me hesitate to get deeper with you, in a way. But also I'm moving forward with this a lot more slowly than you are. I am truly not ready for more than this friendship I have found with you. You're ready for more and you've obviously found it with Trevor, and trust me when I say I am happy for you. Jealous in a way, because I could imagine us together in some future. I kind of wanted to take you to an island and not kill you and bury you, but get to know you. Swing in your hammock with you.*

A cold, empty space opened in Dan's middle. His throat ached. His sinuses burned.

Robin: *But I think I always knew it might not happen. I was honestly surprised you stayed connected with me for as long as you did.*

Dan: *Because I like you, Robin. Do you think...*

Robin: *That we can stay friends?*

Dan: *I feel so cheap.*

Robin: *I think this would be worse if we didn't stay in touch. Like, if you want to.*

Dan: *I do, but it could be weird.*

Robin: *It kinda always was.*

The sound of laugher surprised Dan until he realized it had come from him. Then he felt like weeping again.

Dan: *I'm sorry.*

Robin: *Don't be. The early bird...*

Dan: *Oh no you didn't...*

Robin: *I did.*

Dan: *I actually think Trevor is going to like you. Probably more than I already do. One day we're going to get together and talk metaphor. The three of us. Or the four of us if you want to wait until you find your worm or your bird or... I'm going to stop now.*

Robin: *THANK YOU. For stopping. Also, thanks for the invitation. I'd like that. You know, you were right about that part. About us meeting up as friends and how that would strip away a lot of the expectation. Make it easier for me to connect in person. I'm not immediately balking at this idea.*

Dan: *I'm glad.*

Robin: *So.*

Dan: *So.*

Robin: *Good chat?*

Dan: *Very good chat. Not sure we hit the Gilmore Girls scale, but I feel like we've accomplished something.*

Robin: *Me too. If you don't mind, I think I'm going to end it here, though.*

Dan: *Sure.*

Robin: *If I don't message you back for a few days...*

Dan: *I'll assume you got all tired and took a nap. But when you're feeling up to it, I'll be here. I'm serious. In fact—*

Breaking the golden rule of Let's Connect, Dan entered ten digits.

Dan: *That's my number. Text me. I'm probably going to deactivate my profile in the next few days and I don't want to lose touch.*

Dan's phone buzzed, but no new message popped up on the screen. He swiped down the notification pane and grinned. Robin had texted him.

Robin: *This is me being brave. Now I need to go sleep it off. Take care. Xoxo*

After adding Robin to his contacts—applying a bird avatar rather than the picture Robin had uploaded to the app—Dan deleted Let's Connect. He sat for a moment to let it all sink in, then he tucked his phone into his pocket and went to find Trevor.

The smell of bacon served as his guide, not that he'd get lost in Trevor's small house. But the closer he got to the kitchen, the slower Dan walked as the reality of where he was, how, and why, finally began to sink in. Not that it hadn't earlier. It had—right before his third climax. Waking up naked in Trevor's bed. Having Trevor suggest a shampoo/conditioner combo in the shower.

He was here. They'd... They'd unpacked a box. Perhaps several.

Dan angled his shoulder against the low arch separating the kitchen from the rest of the house and watched Trevor shift from pan to pan, turning bacon and flipping... were those pancakes? A vague mental image of all the other boxes they'd supposedly hidden beneath the floorboards superimposed itself between Dan and Trevor's back. But rather than wince at the suggestion of how much work remained to be done, Dan could only smile.

He didn't care how many boxes were left. Whether unpacking them would prove simple or difficult. The important part was that he and

Trevor would be doing it together. That they should have started earlier almost didn't matter, either. They were here now.

They'd finally connected.

Taking his smile into the kitchen with him, Dan carefully circled Trevor's waist from behind and pressed a kiss to his bristly jawline. "Breakfast for dinner?"

Trevor leaned into him briefly before resuming his flipping and turning. "Seemed appropriate."

"How's that?"

"Better late than never?"

Dan wanted to groan, but a laugh popped out instead. One Trevor returned. Beneath the loose circle of Dan's arms, his belly contracted and shook. Dan hugged him closer for a second before letting go, and Trevor turned, hands and cooking tools upraised as he bent forward for a kiss.

"Appetizer," he murmured.

"Or dessert," Dan whispered back.

Trevor laughed again. "This is going to get old."

"But not for a long, long time."

Then they stood there, grinning at each other, breakfast sizzling, coffee burbling. The wind picking up outside so that snow swirled against the windows. But inside the kitchen, with them dressed in their rattiest sweats, hair all over the place, bellies empty, souls filled, everything was perfect.

Turn the page for an epilogue chapter from Trevor's point of view!

Beach Date

August

With Exit Zero only one mile away, Trevor glanced at his companion and asked the first important question of the day. "Which beach do we want to try?"

Dan frowned. "Oh, um…?"

"Um? Not sure that's an actual beach."

"Jerk. You researched the beaches, didn't you? Why didn't you share this research with me so I could make an informed decision instead of having to decide right now when we're barreling toward an exit and a turnoff?"

Trevor barked a laugh. "Firstly, it's not as if any decision we make is irreversible. We're going to the beach, not the moon. Secondly, yes, I did some research."

"Once a professor, always a professor," Dan muttered.

"Tell me you didn't read reviews for at least six restaurants within walking distance of the B&B."

"Eight, actually. I narrowed our choice to two."

"Mm-hmm."

"Hurry up and tell me about the beaches."

Trevor aimed a pointed look through the windshield and had to squint against the glare of sunlight from the rear window of every other car caught in the mile-long jam with them. He flipped his sunglasses back down from the top of his head to cover his eyes. "I think we've got time."

Dan looked up and groaned. "No kidding. I'd have thought next weekend would be busier."

Next weekend encompassed Labor Day. While Trevor wouldn't have minded ducking away for a couple of days, Dan preferred not to leave his bookstore in the hands of his weekend assistants for longer than absolutely necessary.

The sea of red in front of them rippled, tail lights blinking on and off as traffic crawled forward and stopped again. The dashboard clock clicked another minute toward midday. A quick check of the temperature gauge showed it holding steady. Trevor's Subaru might be nearly as old as he was but it'd hold up to another hour of standing still. Maybe.

Dan had his phone out and was peering at the screen. "Okay, so the closest beach to where we're staying would be… Oh, wait, if we want eye candy, Grant Street is where it's at."

"What's at Grant Street?"

"Lifeguard headquarters."

Trevor shot Dan what he hoped was a droll look. "Really?"

Dan's grin was impish. "I was only thinking of you."

"Mm-hmm."

"Okay, which beach do you recommend? Did you do a chart? Tell me you did a chart."

"I did not do a chart." He'd totally done a chart. Sensibly, he'd left it on his laptop. At home. "Based on the facts I gleaned from a couple of articles, I narrowed it down to two choices."

"Only two?"

"I anticipated this discussion and figured I'd give us less to argue about."

Dan's lips twisted back and forth, as though he was deciding whether or not to pout. Then he pushed out a quick sigh. "Fair enough.

Many a relationship has imploded in a hot car." He leaned toward the dash. "How's Betsy doing, anyway?"

Trevor huffed. "My car's name is not Betsy. And she's doing fine."

Dan patted the dash. "Good old girl. So, beaches."

"If we want less noise and distraction, there's The Point."

Dan stopped stroking the dash long enough to tap the screen of his phone, head bobbing. "Right, that's what it says here."

"If we want the full Cape May experience, we try to find a spot somewhere along Beach Avenue. Like, say near Grant Street."

Dan's grin was back and it did interesting things to Trevor's insides. Not sexual things—though, if he let his mind wander, he'd get there. It was more a lightness around his heart and an easing of the subtle ache between his shoulder blades, both reminding him of how difficult it had become to spend time in Dan's company last year. How easy it was now.

How much everything had changed.

Trevor reached over the center console to take Dan's hand and threaded their fingers together. Smile softening, Dan raised their interlaced fingers to his lips and pressed a kiss to Trevor's knuckles.

The moment held without words until a horn blast reminded Trevor they were in traffic. He eased off the brake and let the car roll forward another car length before slowing again. "Well. We have approximately three hundred more hours to decide between The Point and Grant Street. Any further arguments?"

"Which beach do you want to go to?" Dan asked.

Trevor let his grin bloom and squeezed Dan's hand.

Forty-five minutes later, they'd found a parking spot only a hundred yards from the lighthouse and were trekking toward a more secluded beach along The Point. Shoulders draped with towels and the straps of three separate bags, Dan looked ready for a three-week stay on the sand. Trevor carried only a small cooler, an umbrella, and another towel because he wasn't sure if Dan had plans for all of his. Like perhaps a tent. Or maybe he had a pavilion in one of his bags and cushions in the others.

Trevor stretched his thoughts back a year to the day they'd gone to Wildwood. Had Dan packed a survival kit and too many towels? From memory, they hadn't actually visited the beach. Dan had tried to talk Trevor into getting into one of those huge inflatable beach balls, but that was as close as they'd gotten to the sand. They'd spent the rest of the day on the boardwalk.

He smiled. That had been a fun day. The best, in fact. Though, he suspected the memory shone brighter because of all that had happened afterward.

Trevor had always wondered whether he'd seen the gaps in Dan and Chris's marriage before either Dan or Chris. Or whether they were just better at ignoring the spaces than anyone else. Everything had seemed more brittle that fall, though, and Trevor's semester in California had provided him with the necessary distance to not only let his friends' marriage fail on its own—to not feel as though he was partly responsible—but also to seek out a relationship with someone who could love him back.

He truly hadn't expected to return to the aftermath.

Then again, maybe he had.

Glancing over at Dan now, Trevor experienced another lifting of his heart. For all that his students might like to argue against fate, or the balance of dark against light, Trevor had seen enough of life to know that no one left this planet unscarred. Love wasn't easy—and it shouldn't be. Just as the dark times only made the light shine brighter, finally opening himself to what he really wanted made what he had now all the sweeter.

Dan paused at the end of the sandy path to the beach to look left and right. Trevor followed his gaze, panning left toward a wide expanse of sand dotted with a handful of umbrellas, then right where the umbrellas clustered more closely and the sounds of kids' voices drifted on the breeze. Trevor had hoped the beaches surrounding the Point would be quieter.

At least he wouldn't have to compete for Dan's attention with a tower of stupidly fit lifeguards.

Trevor jerked his head toward the left and Dan nodded in agreement before turning his collection of towels and bags in that direction. They trudged across the sand, skirting the closer umbrellas, passing them, and finding a spot of beach to call their own.

A few minutes later, they were camped beneath a bright circle of fluttering fabric. Trevor reclined on his towel while Dan fussed through his bags. A series of articles landed on the towel spread behind him. Sunscreen, sunglasses, more sunscreen, bug spray, hand sanitizer, two bottles of water, a suspiciously limp and lumpy granola bar—the almond butter had likely melted into a clump at the bottom, leaving the nuts to fend for themselves—a paperback book, two magazines, a plastic container of grapes, a package resembling a poorly wrapped gift which could be anything from medication to something Dan had left in the bottom of his bag two years ago, a dead banana, and a brown paper sack.

"What are you looking for?" Trevor asked.

"This!" Dan turned with a triumphant expression, holding up a package of baby wipes.

He then proceeded to wipe his hands before repacking his bag. One of his bags. Then he stripped off his shirt, balled it up behind his head and flopped back onto his towel.

How could a man who packed hand sanitizer and baby wipes for a day at the beach use a balled-up shirt as a pillow? A sweaty shirt. With buttons.

"What?" Dan said, eyes closed.

"Hmm?"

"I can feel you looking at me."

"Just marveling at one of nature's most contradictory creations."

Dan cracked an eye open. "Do I even want to know what you're talking about?"

"Probably not. Want to go for a swim?"

"Soon. Need to bask for a bit first. Get hot enough to sizzle when I hit the water."

Trevor laughed. "Should probably apply some of that sunscreen."

"Do my back for me?"

"Sure."

If someone were to write the story of their day at the beach, a hush would fall over the scene as Trevor smoothed lotion onto Dan's shoulders and down his back in long sweeps. Dan's skin would already be warm, instead of oddly cold in patches, and he wouldn't have little curls of hair on his shoulders. Three of them on the left and just one on the right, like migratory chest hairs. Neither would Dan be wearing shorts patterned with miniature penguins. Trevor wouldn't be frustrated by the way sand kept getting between his palms and Dan's skin, despite the fact he hadn't touched anything but the sunscreen tube.

There wouldn't be a teenager eyeing them over the top of a portable gaming console or a seagull stalking Trevor's cooler.

But despite the keen un-sexiness of the moment, Trevor could spend eternity there. It hit him while he was squeezing another dollop of sunscreen onto his palm, the tube farting into the gentle breeze. The feeling intensified as he smoothed the lotion down toward Dan's lower back, finding more delicate, misplaced curls—four of them this time—and being able to greet them like old friends. He knew these odd little hairs. He knew Dan's back and the way his hips edged out slightly right there, not in a wide berth because Dan wasn't a large man, but in an interesting and angular way that gave Trevor something to hold on to when they were…

Trevor bit back a groan.

Dan turned his head slightly to murmur, "You're not getting turned on back there, are you?"

"Maybe."

It wasn't just the flash of memory that lit Trevor's fire. It was the weird domesticity of the moment. The tug deep inside his chest. The certainty that this moment could be the perfect moment for his second and arguably most important question of the day.

Then Dan was turning, looking at him, and Trevor lost his nerve.

"Tell me what you're thinking," Dan said.

It was a habit they'd developed over the past few months; one they'd had to institute to get Trevor to verbalize his thoughts. Because, as Dan had explained several times—countless times—telepathy was not a thing.

Trevor swallowed. "I…" He shook his head.

Dan touched his palm to the side of Trevor's face. "Don't do that. I want to know why you looked so dreamy just then."

"Do you ever find yourself overwhelmed by ordinary moments?" Trevor sipped at the air, drawing in a shallow breath as he waited for consternation to crowd Dan's features.

Dan's face wrinkled into a gentle smile instead. "All the time."

"Really?"

"Absolutely. Like the drive down here. Us just being in the car together, companionable, the way we've always been, except I know I get to share a bed with you tonight. Make love. And it'll be some not quite right bed in a room that's not our own. My pillow will be too flat and yours will be lumpy. The sheets won't smell like us. But it'll be a night we remember for a long time because we came away together. Just for one night. We came here together. As a couple. And it's all so corny. I mean… a night at the shore? At the end of summer? But I'm going to love every minute because this is what life is supposed to be. Small moments with the one you love."

Trevor had started nodding halfway through Dan's little ramble. "That's exactly it."

Dan picked up the tube. "Your turn." He made a twirling motion with his hand.

Trevor shrugged out of his shirt, folded it neatly, and set it beside his towel. He swallowed a yelp as cool lotion touched the center of his back. Dan started spreading the sunscreen in quick, efficient moments, but Trevor could feel the attention Dan's fingers paid to his outline in much the same way he'd traced Dan's back. Pausing slightly at points of interest, hesitating at the lower back, where the view must be as familiar to Dan as it had been to Trevor.

A kiss landed on Trevor's shoulder. Dan's voice drifted up toward his ear. "I wish we were alone right now."

Trevor turned. "You wouldn't rather be looking at lifeguards?"

"Not in a million years." Dan nudged Trevor's neck with the tip of his nose. "Want to swim?"

"We just finished putting sunscreen on. We need to set."

"Set?"

Trevor waved a hand. "For, like, ten minutes. So the sunscreen can bond with our skin or whatever."

"Seriously, what planet are you from?"

"The one where skin cancer is a myth."

"You're really not going to go into the water until your sunscreen sets?"

"No, and neither are you."

"But you asked if I wanted to swim before we even did sunscreen."

"Whatever."

"Whatever?" The indignation on Dan's face was adorable.

Trevor grinned. Shrugged. "I forgot then. But now—"

"Stop. Let's just… set."

Dan flopped back into his shirt pillow and Trevor put the sunscreen away. Then he flopped beside his best friend and lover and stared up at the blocks of color over their heads. He felt warm and lazy and enormously content—yet filled with potential, as though he were an electron gathering energy. His second important question pushed upward again but when he turned his head to check on Dan, the question settled back down. Not yet. He wanted to be out in the water when he asked. Inside a moment that included just him and Dan. No idle teenagers. No rapacious seagulls.

"What?" Dan asked, eyes still closed.

"Hmm?"

"I can feel you looking at me again."

"Wondering if you're ready to sizzle."

The side of Dan's mouth crooked upward. "Sure."

Trevor crawled to his feet, feeling less than graceful, and offered Dan a hand up. Dan stood, brushed sand from his hands, and took a step back to look Trevor up and down. "God, you're gorgeous. How are you so damned gorgeous?"

"Stop." Heat not from the sun threatened Trevor's cheeks.

"And so sweet in your bashfulness. Which I'll never get." Dan cocked his head toward the water. "Last one in—"

Trevor took off down the sand and hopped through the water lapping at the shore. The deeper the water, the higher he had to pick up his feet until finally, he settled on wading. When the water crested the waistband of his shorts, he dove into the deep aqua blue, marveling at the way the world could disappear completely the moment water covered his head. One stroke of his arms and he reached the bottom, flattened his palms against the rippled sand, and pushed back upward. The world reinstated itself with a clamorous roar made up of the ocean, the birds, the people on the beach, and the more basic sounds of existence, of life.

After shaking the water out of his hair, Trevor wiped his eyes and looked for Dan… only to find him less than ankle-deep, arms clutched about himself as though the water lapping at his shins was freezing.

"The water really isn't that cold," Trevor called back.

"It sort of is."

"It sort of isn't."

A wave gently buffeted Trevor from behind, rocking him forward onto his toes. The wave continued toward Dan, raising the water to his knees, and Dan's eyes widened slightly. "Okay, maybe it isn't."

He shuffled forward until the water touched the bottoms of his ridiculous shorts, then farther in until his goods were threatened. Another hesitation.

"Just dunk yourself," Trevor suggested. "By the time you finish screaming, you'll be warm."

"Says you." Sucking in a breath, Dan took another few steps, edging his hands down toward his shorts and hissing as another wavelet pushed water up over his waist.

"Hard part's done!"

Dan shot him a weak smile. "It's not that bad out here."

"As I tried to tell you, about twenty times."

"Three times."

"Whatever. C'mere."

Trevor held out a hand and Dan took his fingers. After tugging Dan closer, Trevor turned out toward the ocean and prepared to dive, only to be hauled back upward, Dan making a "Whoa" sound.

"It's like ripping off a bandage!" Trevor said, pushing himself into a sideways dive while tightening his hold on Dan's fingers. Dan wasn't getting out of this one.

Dan splashed down behind him, thrashing about in the water, and Trevor let go. They bobbed back up at the same time and Dan did not look amused. Then he did.

"Bastard."

"You love me," Trevor said.

"I do." Dan grinned a little wider and leaned in for a salty-sweet kiss.

A shiver of apprehension gripped Trevor's shoulders—just lightly. They'd been openly affectionate on the beach without extreme PDA, but a kiss was different. And even though things were better in 2020 than they had been for his first kiss, touching his lips to another man's in a public place always came with a reflexive twitch. The warmth of Dan's lips and the gentleness of the kiss eased his momentary anxiety, and then they were separate beings again, blinking at each other across a small expanse of water.

By mutual consent, they swam out a little farther, until their toes intermittently grazed the floor and the water lapped at their ears.

Another wave lifted Trevor from behind, pushing him slightly forward and into Dan. Trevor took the opportunity to kiss Dan again, caught in the happiest of moments—buoyed by the water, by love, and the simplicity of being here together. A day at the beach with neither of them having to hide how they felt from the other. A day out just for them.

Now, his mind whispered. *Ask him now.*

The ocean floor dropped away from Trevor's feet as a larger wave lifted him and Dan, catching them unaware. Dan let go with a gasp, splashing like a drowning kitten as he searched for footing. Then his head dropped out of view. Trevor reached for him, only to grab an armful of water as the ocean rolled him over sideways and propelled him toward the beach. He skidded along the smooth sand, collecting the top layer with his shorts, and fetched up next to an eroded sandcastle and a surprised child.

Dan crashed into him a second later, spluttering.

The little girl laughed and clapped her hands in delight. The girl's mother arrived the very next second, concern etched across her face.

"Are you guys okay?" she asked.

Trevor tugged at his shorts, which thankfully remained mostly where they should be. "Shorts in place. Check. Yes, I think we're fine."

"The same thing happened to us yesterday," the woman said. "One minute we were bobbing happily out in the waves, the next we were on the beach with sand burns. It's like every tenth swell is a rogue wave or something!"

"Good to know," Dan said, sitting up.

The woman pointed toward the center of the beach. "It's not as bad over there."

"More crowded, though."

She smiled.

Trevor looked at Dan. "Want to go back out? We can swim more toward the middle."

"Sure."

They swam back out, aiming for the center of the beach. They even kissed again. But the moment Trevor had been waiting for, had almost captured, eluded him. For a while, he let it go. Let time drift until they were back beneath their umbrella, sprawled on their backs, panting quietly in the late August heat.

It didn't have to be today, did it? There'd be other trips to the beach, other moments in which he and Dan were the only two people in the world. When the stars felt aligned and invisible birds warbled, and Trevor would feel as though the universe had given him the perfect opportunity to ask Dan to marry him.

Unless those moments never arrived.

Maybe the universe was telling him something else instead. That Dan had tried marriage once and didn't want to try again. That what they had now was good enough. They were living in Trevor's house, waking up together every morning, whispering "sweet dreams" to each other every night. Saturdays were for cooking and Sundays were for watching sports or a movie. They walked the trail at Pennypack with new purpose. They texted back and forth from work. Their lives were so entwined already.

Maybe they didn't need more.

A soft shuffling roused Trevor from a nap he hadn't planned. He blinked at the myriad colors overhead, broad stripes of red, orange, yellow, green… Oh, hey, his umbrella followed the rainbow. Huh. How had he never noticed that before?

Another rustling had his head turning sideways to check out the noise. Dan was fossicking about in his bags again, a small pile of articles behind him. Lifting himself to one elbow, Trevor grabbed a bottle of water. He twisted off the cap and washed sand and salt out of his mouth.

Dan turned. “Hey, sleepyhead.”

“Hey. What are you looking for? I’m pretty sure we left the couch at home. And your favorite pillow.” Dan had a pillow Trevor wasn’t allowed to touch.

Dan resumed his scratching, digging deep into the smallest bag—a fanny pack type thing he’d thankfully not strapped about his waist like a tourist. Then he stilled, as though he’d found something he wasn’t looking for. Like a rat, or a syringe.

“Everything okay?” Trevor asked.

Dan turned back around. “Yep.” He had something in his hand, clutched against his palm.

“What’s up?”

Dan chewed on his lower lip for a few seconds before looking out to sea. Thoroughly confused, which could be due to the nap, Trevor followed his gaze, then looked back at Dan in profile, noting the anxious set of his brow, the tension along his jaw.

Trevor reached out to graze the back of Dan’s balled-up hand. “You’re worrying me.”

Dan looked back at him, then turned his hand over and opened his fingers. “This is for you.”

A silver chain crisscrossed Dan’s palm beneath a pendant in the shape of a gear.

Frowning, Trevor glanced up. “What is this?”

Dan inhaled slowly. “Okay, I’m going to ramble for a few minutes and I might or might not make any sense.”

“Okay.” Trevor’s heart started beating a little faster.

Another breath. “I was watching you sleep—”

"I thought we talked about this."

Dan laughed. "You're the sleeper creeper, not me."

True.

"Anyway." Dan looked down at the necklace. "I saw this online about a month ago and it made me think of you because you're like..." His lower lip disappeared beneath his teeth again. "This is so corny. It's... You're my central gear. For nearly eight years now, you've been the person I turn to when I'm happy or sad. When I need a friend, or when I just want to be." He glanced up. "Us being together, finally... it's working for me. It's like we're two integral parts of a machine. So, I bought the pendant and started planning how to give it to you in a casual way, because except for the day we started down this path, we don't really talk about our feelings, or what we're doing. But I wanted you to know that being with you makes me happy and I think it's going to make me happy for the rest of my life."

"Marry me." Trevor blinked as soon as the words left his lips.

Dan blinked in return.

Trevor opened his mouth to recall his...

Oh my God. He hadn't even asked! He'd issued it like a demand. Birds weren't even singing, damn it. Except for the seagull who still seemed to think Trevor was going to share the contents of his cooler, and— "I mean—"

Dan's face became a blur as he bent forward. Then they were kissing. Quickly. Quietly. Almost furtively. Dan pulled back and Trevor grabbed his shoulder. Pulled him in again. Another rapid kiss.

Then, "I'm—"

Another kiss and Dan whispering close. "Don't you dare say you're sorry, or try to make sense of what you meant."

"So..."

"Yes. I'll marry you."

"I thought—"

"That I might not want to do it again?" Dan shook his head. Drew back and smiled. "At the end of the day, Trev, it's just a piece of paper. It doesn't really mean anything. I mean, yeah, we can have a nice ceremony. Invite our friends to help us celebrate and have an anniversary every year. But it's... It's just a piece of paper. The important part is you and me and this moment."

This moment.

"If you'd never asked, it wouldn't have mattered. But..." Dan's expression turned wistful. "I'd be lying if I said I'm not glad you did."

Trevor had managed to sit up. Leaning forward, he touched Dan's fingertips. "If I hadn't asked, would you have? Is that what the pendant was for?"

"Maybe? Kind of. It felt too soon to declare forever but I wanted to anyway."

Dan held out the chain and Trevor took it. Smiled as he stroked the buffed metal edges of the gear, admiring the sturdy nature, the width of the little teeth, and the evenness all the way around.

"Will you show me where you got this?" he asked.

Dan nodded. "Sure."

"I want to get something for you too." Emotion hit him then, and for a second, Trevor marveled that he'd gotten this far without choking up. Dan had said *yes*. He'd asked and Dan had said *yes*.

It shouldn't make a difference. Dan was right. What they already shared was perfect. But the idea of linking their lives officially, their names, made Trevor happy in a way he had no words for.

Almost whispering, he said, "I'd like to get rings, too."

Dan's hand edged into view, his fingertips coming to rest beside Trevor's. Trevor looked up from the pendant.

"We should absolutely get rings," Dan said.

Trevor swallowed. "Okay. We need to talk about something else now because I'm about to cry on a public beach."

"Can't have that."

"God, no."

"Want to swim again? You could cry out there and no one would ever know."

Trevor gazed out at the ocean and smiled. Nodded. "Let's do that."

He tucked the pendant away inside his folded shirt and stood. Held out a hand to Dan. Felt a click, or perhaps the seating of one gear against another as Dan's hand slid into his. Completeness surrounded him for a moment, as though the connection between their hands had activated a bubble to enclose just them. Trevor squeezed Dan's fingers for a second before tugging him forward. He took one step, then two, then ran toward the water, splashing in without waiting for Dan to say it was cold or to shiver by the shore. He pulled Dan in deeper with him, almost hoping for a rogue wave to toss them together and tangle them up on the sand.

A happy yell exploded from Trevor's chest as the surf crashed into him. Planting his feet, he looked up at the blue sky, tipping his head back so that the sun could blind him, and yelled again.

Dan slid an arm around his waist, skin hot and cold at the same time, and Trevor leaned in close.

"Happy?" Dan asked.

"Very."

"Good."

"Love you," Trevor said, slinging his arm around Dan's shoulders.

"Love you too," Dan said.

And there it was. Simple as that. Together. The deed done. Light. Free. Happy.

With this day officially becoming the best day.

This day was everything.

Wondering what's next for Robin? He has a story too! Read on for a sneak peek at the first chapter of *Let's Go Out*

Let's Go Out

(Let's Connect, Book Two)

The Front Door

At first, the new requests lighting up the Let's Connect chat app were flattering. Now that Robin had replaced the small bird he'd been using as an avatar with an actual photo of himself, people wanted to talk to him! But as he scrolled through the shortish list, his spirits dipped, dragged along the floor, and finally slipped between the cracks. It wasn't the sameness of the dating profiles attached to each request—though they were startlingly similar. It was that he'd been waiting eight hours for one particular person to comment.

A confirmed citizen of the digital world, Robin had learned not to read too much into online communication. Text didn't always convey the same meaning as face-to-face conversation. Internet connections dropped. Phones broke. But, damn. It'd been eight hours since he'd uploaded the photo, and Dan had yet to respond.

Had Dan's connection dropped? Was his phone broken? A foot of snow covered the ground outside. Dan couldn't possibly have gone out, could he? Maybe he had, and had forgotten his phone?

Or the roof of his shop or whatever had fallen in.

Or he'd been caught out during the snow and now had hypothermia.

Or…

Maybe this was what ghosting felt like.

With an imaginary rope tying anxious knots in his gut, Robin flipped back to his profile on the app to check out his picture. Small, at first, then full size.

He looked okay. He'd thought about taking his glasses off, but figured that since he quite literally could not see his hand in front of his face without them—not to count the fingers, anyway—he should leave them on. His eyes didn't appear too myopic behind the lenses. Or weirdly small. The brown of his irises showed well. It was a nice color, wasn't it?

Robin flashed back to the time he'd wanted green eyes, because green eyes were different. Exciting? He'd ordered colored contacts and gone out to face the world through a haze of green—not that the contacts colored his vision, just his perception. Feeling new, or reinvented, he'd met someone and gone home with him, only to be booted to the curb before the wet spot had dried in the sheets they'd tangled together.

But, hey, he'd managed to have sex with someone real. That should have counted as a win.

The jury was still out. So were the lenses, which remained boxed and stacked in the darkest corner of a cupboard in the bathroom.

Eyes refocused on his photo, Robin brushed a hand over the top of his head. His hair was necessarily short (the explanation for which he probably wouldn't be getting into), his beard neat, both liberally sprinkled with gray. He was forty-nine and lucky to have any brown left at all.

Was it his nose? At eight, his mother had assured him that God had given him the nose he'd needed to hold his glasses in place. Neither the size of his schnoz nor the weight of his new glasses had seemed particularly holy.

At eighteen, Robin had still been growing into his nose.

At twenty-eight, he'd felt he had. Or, at the very least, that the angularity of the beak in the middle of his face matched the gawkiness of the rest of his frame.

At thirty-eight, Robin had wondered, briefly, whether the date who'd booted him to the curb had lied about liking his nose.

At forty-nine, he barely thought about it—or he hadn't *until now.*

His phone trilled a bright cadence of notes, snapping Robin back to the present. He checked the new notification and nearly dropped the phone. Dan had finally messaged him—which of course meant Robin had to spend the next sixty seconds thinking about anything else and failing.

The rope in Robin's gut rolled and tightened, pulling all of his intestines into a confused bundle as he swiped down and read the text.

Dan: *So, guess what? You look like you. I didn't have a complete mental picture, not a physical one, anyway. But your photo totally matched who I thought I was talking to. I'm going to say that's a win. I'm also going to say that I get being shy. Honestly, I do. But this picture is going to make a huge difference to your profile. I bet you've already had a bunch of new connection requests.*

Text didn't always convey the same meaning as face-to-face conversation but Dan's tone was pretty clear. That last line? Not actually in bold text, but Robin had a hard time seeing anything before it, because that last line meant whatever they'd been building together was about to come down.

The rope inside Robin's gut fell loose, leaving him disconcerted and slightly nauseated. But he managed a response.

Robin: *Uploading an actual picture of myself turned out to be a low-key event.*

Sort of, except for the almost panic attack.

Robin: *I spent all night tossing and turning—*

A fact he apparently had to share with Dan?

Robin: *—and then I posted it and the world didn't explode. Funny about that. And, yes, I did get new connection requests today. Guess I'm not paper bag material after all.*

Dan wanted to know whether he truly thought he was, and Robin had to admit he didn't, not really, but it was a thing people said, wasn't it? When they didn't know what else to say. When they'd figured out a conversation was going one way, even though they'd hoped it might go another.

Robin's conversation with Dan went the one way.

Dan was kind, as he always was, but he had a confession to make. One Robin had been expecting ever since the first mention of Dan's BFF, Trevor, during an early chat. Last night, while Robin took and retook his picture, trying to find an expression that said approachable but not needy, Dan and Trevor had figured out their differences.

Now they were together.

Robin tried to be gracious about it. He kept his replies upbeat, his tone light. But inside, his loosed innards were withering and dying. Nausea was no longer a concern. Instead, the fatigue that shrouded the end of anxious episodes descended, wrapping his shoulders in a heavy embrace. The phone in his palm turned into a ten-pound weight. The light cascading through the window became a flash of horror in a dark world.

Dan ended the chat with his cellphone number and an invitation to coffee.

Every instinct Robin had urged him to ignore both. It would be easier to become the ghost.

Then he made himself switch from the Let's Connect app to his phone's text app. Whether it was a desire to put a mark on Dan's phone that might send a prick of guilt in Dan's direction every time he saw it, a need to preserve what had started to feel like a friendship, a jibe at himself, or a call to action no one but Robin might understand, he entered Dan's number and typed:

This is me being brave. Now I need to go sleep it off.

✉

The sun interrupted Robin's backward slump into naptime. He'd lifted his feet from the floor with the intent of nestling his toes into the blanket bunched at the far end of the couch. He'd tilted his head toward his favorite pillow.

The sun, careless of his plans for an afternoon nap, hit him full in the face.

Robin squinted toward the window. Stupidly, he'd drawn the curtains back to peer out at the snow, and now the sun had moved far enough west to peek out from behind the houses on the opposite side of the street.

Uttering a cross between a sigh and a moan, Robin pushed up off the couch, slid his feet into slippers, and went to close the curtains. Before dragging them across the window, though, he peered out. Cold radiated from the glass, reflecting the snow blanketing his small front yard. Higher piles of snow to either side hid the shrubs marking the borders between his house and his neighbors'. The walk was clear, and beyond the three steps leading down to the street, the snow had been pushed away from the sidewalk to form a long battlement between him and Kerper Street.

Being a Sunday afternoon, it was quiet out. Robin studied the wall of snow along the street and the narrow passage across his front yard.

The last words he'd texted to Dan drifted across his mind.

This is me being brave.

He could go out there. The space was limited. Contained.

He could… He could go out there. Turn his face into the sun, breathe in the scent of snow.

Robin was squinting toward the far end of the street, when a shadow bounced into the corner of the front window. Swallowing a yelp, Robin stumbled backward. The coffee table met his calves and he sat. At the window, a pair of hands framed a curious face topped by a crown of dark fluffy hair. Kaleb, the son of his next-door neighbor, was growing his curls into an afro and spent more time fussing with his hair than breathing.

Spying Robin, Kaleb grinned and waved. He then pulled out his pick.

Robin put a hand to his heart. It could have been worse. The man in the window could have been Kaleb's father, Sean.

Sean was…

Robin couldn't handle Sean today. Not with ropes and things slithering around inside him.

Kaleb knocked on the glass and pointed toward the door. Then, perhaps assuming Robin hadn't gotten the message, he knocked on the door.

Robin got up again and opened the door. Kaleb's smile—as bright as the snow bunched around the stoop—lent Robin the strength to curve his own lips for a minute or two. For long enough to see what Kaleb wanted.

Hand out, palm upward, Kaleb got to the point. "Got any cash? I know we usually settle up on Mondays, but there's this drum set on sale, and Dad's in project mode and Herc and I want to go see it and if we have all the money with us, we could buy it today." Kaleb glanced down. "Floor looks good." He cocked his head. Fussed with his hair. "Can I use your car?"

Robin watched as Kaleb teased out a few curls and patted them into place, before he asked, "How much do I owe you?"

Kaleb indicated the small piles of snow to either side of the door. "Including the shoveling? Say, fifty?"

He could ask for three times that and Robin would pay. For services rendered, Kaleb was worth his weight in green paper.

Robin went in search of his wallet. Kaleb trailed him into the house, letting the screen door slam behind him. The front door whispered closed a second later, followed by the sound of someone who wasn't quite an adult but who wanted to sound like one slapping his hands together and saying, "Sure is a cold one out there today."

Robin grunted in acknowledgment. His wallet was where it usually was—with his mail, keys, and other pocket detritus, all lined up along the counter-height pass-through between the dining room and the kitchen, both of which faced the living room, making the first floor of his town house both cozy and functional.

"How much do you need for the drums?"

As though the house next-door didn't produce enough sound. Sean was a mosaic artist and kept a kiln in a shed out back. It wasn't the baking part of the process that made noise, though. It was the *tink*, *tink*, *tink*, of Sean's tools as he carved shapes into and out of the tiles he made. And the curious *thumps* at odd hours Robin hadn't quite identified. The music while he worked. Plus the sounds of two people going about their day.

They apologized once a year, on Thanksgiving.

Sean and Kaleb had arrived next door about a year before Robin's ex had departed. Robin's ex had been more social than Robin, and a plan for Thanksgiving had cropped up between the four of them—seeing as none of them apparently had anywhere else to go or anyone else to celebrate with.

When they'd shown up the second year with a dish of something and a bottle of something, Robin had been surprised. He wasn't completely antisocial, but it often took him a while to work up to being talkative. And friendly. Normal? Sociable.

Robin glanced up from his wallet at the boy standing in front of him. At the young man who was old enough to drive. "Where are these drums?"

"Oxford Avenue. Over by the cemetery."

Nodding absently, Robin pulled out the single twenty hidden in his billfold. "Is this going to be enough? I can Venmo the rest, but I don't know how long a transfer takes on a weekend."

"Nah, this is good." The twenty disappeared and the hand reappeared. "Keys?"

Robin passed them over. "You might want to warm her up a bit before you go out."

"Okay. So, what's next?" Kaleb was studying the floor again. He shifted his attention to the kitchen nook. "Are you going to do in there?"

Robin followed Kaleb's gaze and curled his lip at the cracked and stained linoleum. All things considered, the town houses in the Oxford Circle neighborhood of Philadelphia had weathered their years pretty well—on the outside. Inside was a different story, and mostly dependent upon the decorating decisions of previous owners and tenants. Robin had owned his place for close to ten years, and over the past three he'd been slowly updating the floors and fixtures, starting with the basement and working his way upward. He'd nearly finished the first floor. He only had the kitchen floor and cabinets to go. Then he'd paint the walls and move his tools upstairs.

"Should I do the cabinets first, do you think?" he asked. "That way if I drop a door, I won't damage a new floor."

Kaleb shrugged. "Like, how heavy is a cabinet door? Or are you going to do the counters too? Maybe some of that marble stuff or concrete or whatever?"

"I haven't decided yet." Energy for his years-long project came in fits and starts. Inspiration too.

"Let me know. Whatever I can pick up for you, I will."

Robin found another smile. "Thanks."

"Whatever." Taken out of context, Kaleb's reply might seem callous. Robin knew better. Kaleb was Robin's window on the world. Without Kaleb, well, they both knew the score.

"Did you text me a grocery list yet?" Kaleb asked, pulling out his phone.

"Sorry, no. I've been busy."

"New game or are you still working on *Wyrmkind*?"

"That. Yes." Much easier to let Kaleb think all Robin had on his mind was work. "I'll text you a list in the morning." Robin grasped for a different conversational straw. "How's school?"

Kaleb shrugged one shoulder. "It's school."

"Any more thoughts on what you're going to do next year?"

"Maybe the band will make it big." Kaleb's grin was full of the optimism only a seventeen-year-old could muster.

"The band." There was going to be more than drums?

Also, would this band mean Kaleb would have less time to be Robin's window on the world?

Kaleb jerked his head toward the basement stairs. "Mind if I head out this way? I'll get the car started before I run back home for my keys and stuff."

"Sure."

Robin followed Kaleb downstairs to the half-basement he used as an office and workshop. He'd spent the better part of a year renovating the space, and loved how it made him feel: safe, nested, and yet still professional.

He'd constructed all the furniture (minus the chair) himself. After months of scanning catalogs for exactly what he'd wanted, building the desk-height countertops had proven easier and less expensive. They ran the length of two of the walls, meeting in one corner. Robin designated that corner the nerve center, but computers and monitors crowded both counters. He'd also built the bookshelves hugging the remaining two walls. The middle of the room had been left clear for the chair that had cost about the same as a fully upgraded gaming rig. Damn good chair, though. Robin had been rolling along the length of both counters in it for about six months now with no complaints.

Sometimes Kaleb hung out with him in the basement, Robin at one computer Kaleb at another (using a kitchen chair and complaining about the fact he never got to drive the "Porsche"). They'd game until Sean realized no one had interrupted him from wherever he was or until Robin realized no one had interrupted him and Kaleb from wherever they were. Sometimes Kaleb was the one who remembered humans needed to eat and sleep and all of that.

It was an amicable arrangement.

Today, Kaleb bypassed all of the computers without a glance—obviously following the siren beat of his "new" drums. He disappeared into the garage. Robin followed and smacked the door release. The door groaned as it rose along the tracks. Once it was open, he nodded at Kaleb, who was already behind the wheel of Robin's twenty-year-old Toyota hatchback. The car only Kaleb ever drove.

The engine coughed and caught.

"Watch for ice!" Robin called.

Kaleb gave him a wave.

Robin ducked back inside the house and climbed the stairs. In the living room, he peeked at the couch, but his momentum had been broken. His fatigue had disappeared. If he tried for a nap, he'd only lie on the couch thinking about Dan. Or Sean.

Ugh.

He considered the window instead and thought about the wall of snow bordering the street. The apparent safety of the front yard.

And shivered.

Turning about, Robin jogged back downstairs and started turning on monitors. He wanted snow and sunshine? He could sketch out some ideas for a new environment for *Wyrmkind.* Or, just, you know, play for a while. Spend long enough in a virtual world and it often started to feel real.

That was what he told himself, anyway.

Dan's Curry Recipe

This creamy lentil curry is so good! Now, you may be thinking *lentils*? (Or you may be thinking, yay, lentils!) Trust me, this dish is so rich and hearty, you won't miss the meat. But I can imagine chicken would work well with the creamy sauce. Just add any cooked meat in around the time you'd add the lentils to the sauce (toward the end of step three).

In case you're wondering where the ghee is, you don't actually need any for this recipe. I threw that line into the story because it sounded fun. Also, if Robin was going to grind his own coriander and mustard seeds, he'd totally teach himself how to clarify butter!

INGREDIENTS

2/3 cup dry brown lentils
2 green chiles (jalapeno or serrano, depending on how much heat you'd like), sliced thin
1 1-inch piece of ginger, sliced into thin strips or grated
½ cup melted, unsalted butter
¾ cup crushed tomatoes[1]
½ teaspoon cayenne
1 teaspoon ground coriander
¾ teaspoon crushed, dried fenugreek leaves[2]
7 cloves of garlic, finely chopped
½ cup heavy cream
Salt
Extra ginger for garnish

NOTES

1) Pureed diced tomatoes would work, but tomato sauce is too sweet.

2) Fenugreek can be hard to find. Good substitutes are maple syrup, lightly toasted mustard seeds, or curry powder. I've used a ¾ teaspoon of Dijon mustard and it worked beautifully!

INSTRUCTIONS

1) Rinse the lentils, picking out any grit, and add them a small pot with 1½ cups of fresh water. Bring to a boil. Skim any scum from the surface of the water, then strain the lentils and return them to the pot. Add a fresh water, green chiles, and ginger. Simmer, covered, for 15 minutes.
2) Add ¼ cup of the butter and simmer on low heat for another 15 minutes (or until the lentils become tender). Stir often, and as the lentils soften, mash them with the back of a spoon.
3) Melt the remaining ¼ cup of butter in a deep, nonstick pan. Add the tomato puree and sauté on low heat until fat rises to the surface. Add the cayenne, ground coriander, fenugreek (or substitute), and garlic and cook for a couple of minutes, stirring constantly, until the mixture begins to dry and stick to the pan. Add the lentils and stir in. Add the cream and stir in well. Add a cup of water and salt to taste. Bring to a boil.
4) Serve hot, garnished with fresh ginger.

Enjoy!

Dear Reader

Thank you for reading *Let's Connect*. I hope you enjoyed the story. If so, would you consider leaving a review? Reader reviews help independent authors gain exposure and I appreciate every single one.

To talk about books, join us in my Facebook reader group, **Kelly's Keepers**.

Not on Facebook? For new release news, sales, exclusive giveaways, and all the extras, subscribe to my newsletter at:
http://eepurl.com/czGhYz

Acknowledgments

I've long wanted to write a serial for my newsletter subscribers. They're an amazing group of people who faithfully open every missive from me, even when all I have to report is all the writing I haven't been doing.

I wanted to deliver a fresh installment of this serial weekly, so I decided to create a set of events that would feel episodic. I'm a novelist, though, and I couldn't help linking Dan's dating adventures into a larger narrative—and finding him a happy ever after. That his "one" wasn't the person originally intended shouldn't have surprised me. I may not always understand what my characters want. They always do.

So, my first thanks go out to Dan, Robin, and Trevor for allowing me to tell their story—Trevor in particular for hanging out on the sidelines until the time was right.

My second thanks go to my newsletter subscribers. If they hadn't loved this novella, you wouldn't be reading it.

Thank you to my beta readers, Jenna Kendrick and Sahar Abdulaziz. Your comments and insights helped shape this final version, especially when it came to making Trevor's intentions a little clearer.

Thank you to Alex Whitehall for the copy edits. I always appreciate your attention to detail.

Thank you to Natasha Snow for this gorgeous cover!

Thank you to Marie for the illustrations that bring my characters to life.

And, finally, thank you to you, my readers, for being there, and for encouraging me to keep writing.

About the Author

If aliens ever do land on Earth, Kelly will not be prepared, despite having read over a hundred stories of the apocalypse. Still, she will pack her precious books into a box and carry them with her as she strives to survive. It's what bibliophiles do.

Kelly is the author of twelve novels—including the Chaos Station series, co-written with Jenn Burke—and several novellas and short stories. Some of what she writes is speculative in nature, but mostly it's just about a guy losing his socks and/or burning dinner. Because life isn't all conquering aliens and mountain peaks. Sometimes finding a happy ever after is all the adventure we need.

Connect with Kelly online:
https://kellyjensenwrites.com/

Facebook
https://www.facebook.com/kellyjensenwrites/

Twitter
@kmkjensen

Other Titles by Kelly Jensen

Out in the Blue
Wrong Direction
When Was the Last Time
Best in Show
Block and Strike
To See the Sun

The Let's Connect Series
Let's Connect
Let's Go Out

The This Time Forever series
Building Forever
Renewing Forever
Chasing Forever

The Aliens in New York series
Uncommon Ground
Purple Haze

The Counting series
Counting Fence Posts
Counting Down
Counting on You

The Chaos Station series
(with Jenn Burke)
Chaos Station
Lonely Shore
Skip Trace
Inversion Point
Phase Shift

www.ingramcontent.com/pod-product-compliance
Lightning Source LLC
LaVergne TN
LVHW091002080826
845145LV00003B/1091

* 9 7 8 1 9 5 0 6 2 5 1 3 0 *